"Is there

This was her room and she wasn't about to leave. "What do you want now?" she demanded. Jace had a full bottom lip that cried out to be nibbled on. She was startled by her own thoughts—she'd *never* thought that way before!

"We need to work on our relationship."

"No."

"You really are beautiful."

"No." With a slowness that was torturous, her heart pounding in her ears, his parted mouth grazed hers then pulled away.

"I want you." The words seemed torn from him, and he was kissing her like she'd always wanted to be kissed.

A moan echoed in the room and she wasn't sure if it came from her or Jace. *This was a man who hated women. This was a man she had decided to stay away from!* She barely had enough strength to say the word. "Yes."

Rita Clay Estrada, cofounder and first president of the Romance Writers of America, didn't start out to be a writer. She studied art and psychology, worked as a model, a secretary, a salesperson and a bookstore manager. But Rita's countless fans are glad she found her true calling—creating enthralling romances. *The Lady Says No* is her tenth book for the Harlequin Temptation line. This talented author makes her home in Texas.

Books by Rita Clay Estrada

The Lady
Says No
RITA CLAY ESTRADA

Harlequin Books

TORONTO • NEW YORK • LONDON
AMSTERDAM • PARIS • SYDNEY • HAMBURG
STOCKHOLM • ATHENS • TOKYO • MILAN

For Anne and Tom Veitch,
good people and good friends.
And for Frank,
for so many reasons....

Published June 1991

ISBN 0-373-25449-0

THE LADY SAYS NO

1

"WHAT DO YOU HAVE against Gina O'Con as a sister-in-law?" Alicia sipped her gin and tonic as she eyed the ruggedly handsome man across the small cocktail table. Her drink was perfectly made. So was the man.

"What makes you think I have anything against Gina?" he asked.

"I can understand Brad coming to the opening of Gina's hotel. After all, she borrowed the money to renovate the place from him. And she's going to marry him. But you and Cam being here doesn't make sense. Since when do *all* the wealthy and influential Bartholomew brothers show up at an opening of a hotel?" she demanded. "I'd say you all thought your brother needed a champion. Or a bodyguard."

"Brad doesn't need any of those things. We're here to give Gina moral support."

"Right," Alicia stated dryly. "Or is it to check out the woman Brad is in love with and see if you can change his mind about her?"

Jace Bartholomew shrugged his broad shoulders. "If Gina is what Brad wants, then their relationship is fine by me." His blue-eyed gaze never left her face.

She raised her brows. "No more heckles and jeers from the peanut gallery?"

"I never heckled her," he corrected firmly, his full mouth turning into a thin line. "I told Brad weeks ago that I was behind whatever he decided. It was our

mother who held a grudge—one that should have been
buried long ago. My brother knows that, Alicia."

Her shoulders relaxed a little, the defensiveness dis-
sipating. Gina O'Con was her best friend, and as long
as the Bartholomew family was the slightest bit antagonistic, Alicia Dumont would remain protective of her.

She was also very familiar with the story of how Mrs.
Bartholomew had tried to ruin Brad and Gina's relationship because her husband had had an affair with
Gina's mother. The affair, if it could be called that, had
lasted almost twenty years, because Brad's mother
would not grant her husband the divorce he had begged
for. Finally, Mrs. Bartholomew's quest for revenge had
driven her over the edge. She was in a mental hospital
in Dallas. So, while her family was now free of her ma-
nipulations, her sons still bore the scars of the wounds
their mother had inflicted.

Alicia and Jace had retreated to the bar to escape
from the crush of people attending the opening night
of the Casa Mañana Hotel in the River Oaks section of
Houston. As the hotel's decorator, Alicia was thrilled
that the guests—including Jace Bartholomew—had
been impressed by her work.

Jace would soon be Gina's brother-in-law, if Alicia
was reading the signs right. He was a powerhouse of a
man, a mover and shaker in the business community
and a heartbreaker among women. Even as Alicia admitted that he was one of the most attractive men she
had ever met, she reminded herself that he lived in
Chicago, Illinois. Her home base was in San Francisco, California.

Thank goodness.

She took another sip of her drink.

"You're a very beautiful woman." Jace's voice was without inflection. No admiration. No wonder. Not even flattery. *Just the plain facts, ma'am.* "But I'm sure you've been told that often enough."

"Thank you." She almost choked, and decided to ignore his last remark. "And you're a very handsome man," she added in the same monotone he'd used.

For the first time that evening he smiled. It was breathtaking, dammit. "Thank you." Then he frowned into his scotch.

She sighed in relief.

Then he stared at her again and tension once more tightened her body. "I want you to do me a favor."

Alicia narrowed her eyes. Big men like him usually asked big favors, but they also used charm while asking. This man didn't. If this conversation was any indication, he was blunt and to the point. That alone made her wary.

"It depends," she hedged. "Personal or business? Paid or for charity?" No matter what the favor, she already knew the answer. It would be no. Jace Bartholomew was out of her league. Actually most men were, since there wasn't one around who didn't have more experience at this sort of thing than she did. But she couldn't ignore Jace's sexual magnetism. Even as she was drawn to him, she hated it.

Hormones, Alicia. That's all that's calling to you. Pure hormones. Latin, from the word horny. She smiled at her wayward thoughts. Until this moment she had never had firsthand experience of what the word meant. But she'd bet her life savings that it was exactly what she was experiencing right this minute.

"I want you to decorate the Bartholomew Building in Chicago. It's an old building built in the twenties and has unlimited possibilities, but at this point it's an antiquated mess."

"Why me?"

"Because you're one of the few decorators I know who could give it an air of professionalism along with the warmth and old-world charm the building deserves. I've seen your work. You're better than good. You're excellent."

It was tempting. She shook her head. "I'm sorry. I can't."

His gaze pinned her to the spot. When he spoke again, Alicia was relieved. "You'll be well paid, I assure you."

She stared back. "I always am, Mr. Bartholomew."

"Then what's the problem?"

"I'm already committed for the next year." It was a lie, but she didn't care. Working with a man she was physically attracted to was not the thing to do. Especially not with this man.

"You are not," he told her softly. "I called your secretary and she said you were free for the next few months."

"She was wrong," Alicia snapped, angry at being caught out and even angrier that her new secretary didn't know when to keep her mouth closed. "When did you call her?"

"About forty-five minutes ago. Although it was seven-thirty here in Houston, it's only five-thirty in San Francisco, and she was just about to leave the office. She was even kind enough to give me the number where you could be reached. This hotel, of course."

"Of course." She'd have to speak with her secretary. No information was to be given out without permission. Ever. A mistake like this could be dangerous.

"Will you at least consider it?"

"I'm sorry. I can't."

Jace leaned back in his chair. "Are you afraid of me, Alicia?"

"No." Her tone was firm, she hoped.

"Are you attracted to me? Is that the problem?"

She straightened. "Sure of yourself, aren't you?"

"I know what I look like, if that's what you mean." He spoke with a casual, matter-of-fact air. "I also know that my money is a hell of a big attraction. Most women say yes because they think they can change my mind about marriage. Or they say no because they can't stand the heat of competition. They're afraid of being just one more in a long line of females."

Her drink hit the table a little harder than she intended. "My, my. And I thought your younger brother, Cam, was the conceited one in the family."

Continuing to study her, he appeared to ignore her comment. "In your case, I'd say you feel the same sexual pull between us that I do, and you're afraid of it—or me."

He leaned forward and she almost pulled back. Almost. "Although you're one of the most savvy women I've met in business, I'd say your personal life is a little on the naive side."

She couldn't deny it, but was damn sure not going to acknowledge it! "And I'd say you're searching in the dark. I said no to your business proposal. I meant no. Is this one of the few times in your life you've heard the word?"

"One of the few," he acknowledged, as if it was no big deal. "But I don't usually take no for an answer. Not in business."

Alicia downed the last of her drink. He had no way of knowing that her refusal had taken all her strength and willpower. "Thank you for the drink, Mr. Bartholomew. It tasted as bad as quinine, just like this meeting. If I were suffering from malaria, the cure would be worth the discomfort. But I'm not. And this is no longer a cozy little chat in the confines of a dark, romantic hotel bar, so I'll take my leave."

"Where do you discuss business, Alicia?"

"In my office between the hours of nine to five. Just like most businessmen."

"Uh, uh," he corrected her. "Most businessmen do what we're doing now. Only women take the offer of a drink as a proposal of something more intimate."

Jace leaned back again, his smile curling his lips—in disdain? "Just like you, Alicia. One drink doesn't lead to a toss in the hay. At least not with me."

Alicia dropped her purse, placed her hands upon the table and leaned toward him, willing fire into her hazel eyes. "One drink doesn't buy you the right to a favor, either—in business or in bed. At least not with me."

A glimmer of admiration shone in his blue eyes for a moment, then it was gone. "Running away is always easier than confronting the problem, isn't it?"

"I run as fast and as far away as I can from boors, rude men and supposed *business* proposals," Alicia stated in a low, angry voice. She stood up, then stared at him disdainfully. "That's why I'm running from you and your suggestion."

Her back ramrod straight, she walked from the bar and into the lobby. Her hands shook, and no matter where she looked, she saw his face. Maybe she should draw a picture of him and stick it on her dart board at work. He'd be the perfect target. . . .

She stopped. Most of the guests in the lobby were standing in a semicircle around a shimmering sheet of water cascading down a huge brass-covered wall. Flashbulbs were going off and Graham Bartholomew, head of the Bartholomew Corporation, was speaking.

"This evening is one of the most wonderful nights of my life. I have two very important announcements to make. One is that as of the first of the month I am retiring. And this time I mean it."

That provoked a smattering of laughter, and even Alicia had to smile. Jace's uncle had retired from the position of chairman of the board of Bartholomew Corporation twice before and threatened to do so at least a dozen times over the past decade. But something in his voice made her believe that this time it was for good.

"I'm handing the reins to my oldest nephew, Brad Bartholomew, who has been doing the work without the title for the past several years, anyway. So this announcement is just a formality for our dear friends and the press." Graham lifted his champagne flute. "So here's to Brad. May he enjoy the job as much as I'll enjoy watching him."

Several shouts of encouragement rose above the thunderous applause. Alicia couldn't see Brad, but she knew he would be standing beside his uncle. And her friend Gina would be with him.

As the clapping died down, Graham raised his glass again. "And now another announcement that gives me as much pleasure as my retirement," he declared in a loud, booming voice. There was a sudden silence. "On the night of her triumphant opening—of this hotel— one that will be the queen of the Bayou City once again—Gina O'Con has just agreed to become a permanent fixture in the Bartholomew Corporation. She has consented to marry my nephew, Brad Bartholomew."

Tears of joy filmed Alicia's eyes as she joined in the clapping and yelling. Gina deserved this happiness. And Brad, as was apparent for everyone to see, was deeply in love with her. They would live happily ever after.

Wasn't that every girl's dream? At least until they grew into women and were hit with a major dose of reality. It had been Alicia's, too—until she'd grown up.

Long ago, when she was in college, she'd been blindly, head over heels in love. Her handsome law-school fiancé had been everything she'd ever dreamed of. An only child, she'd always been competitive, willing to go the extra mile to get ahead. And Tony had been the same way, or so she'd thought. But Tony's competitiveness had led him down a different path. He'd wooed her into their engagement, spinning cotton-candy dreams. Their life would be wonderful, he an attorney and she a world-famous decorator. But while he was weaving his fantasy web around her, he'd also been busy convincing every girl on campus to become his partner in a bed. He'd even kept track of his conquests, marking notches on the sport calendar that hung on the kitchen wall.

When Alicia caught him, however, he wasn't in bed making love. She'd let herself into his apartment and, hearing noises, had halted in the middle of the living room. Unwilling to believe her ears, she'd heard him getting dressed and calmly telling a sobbing girl that although she was sweet and hot in the sack, that was as far as their relationship could go. In a daze Alicia had gone into the bedroom, where the "sweet and hot" girl was still in bed naked, crying her blue eyes out.

That had made two women crying their eyes out in the same room at the same time over the same man.

Realizing that she'd made a very bad choice of a fiancé, Alicia had decided not to choose again for a while. She didn't trust herself to choose wisely. So she'd aimed all her energy elsewhere. The need to further her career became all-consuming. There was no room for men in her life unless they were clients.

And each time she felt herself succumbing to manly charms, she remembered that scene in Tony's bedroom. And she never again cried over a man.

"They really will be good for one another." Jace's voice was soft and low in her ear, ever so warm. He was standing directly behind her.

She stiffened, but refused to move. "Yes, they are. But I didn't expect you to be capable of knowing that. I'm stunned by your perception."

He chuckled and a burst of excitement shocked her nerves into awareness. "No, you're not. I told you earlier I was in favor of this match. Brad is in love with her. And until they're married, he's worthless to the corporation."

"How kind of you. And all this time I thought you were against the institution of marriage." She laced her words with sarcasm.

"I am. But only for me. I wouldn't presume to tell my brothers how to lead their lives. I only decide about my own."

"Right," she drawled, all but calling him a liar.

She wanted to face him, to shout at him. To hold him close. Her conflicting emotions were warring with her principles. He was trouble. So why was she drawn to him? She thought she'd outgrown her tendency to pick out the worst of men and find him sweet.

"You're awfully wary." His warm breath brushed her cheek and a shiver went down her spine. "Still running?"

"You bet." Without looking back, she walked straight ahead to the bank of elevators. She knew Jace was staring at her. She felt his eyes stabbing her between the shoulder blades like daggers.

When she got into the elevator, Alicia turned her back on the glass front overlooking the lobby. Jabbing at the buttons, she held her breath until the door closed and the climb to the third floor began.

She was going to bed. Now. Before she got into trouble. After all, this past week she hadn't been able to go to bed until two or three every morning. And when dawn hit her window, she was up and running again. She was exhausted and this was a perfect time to catch up on her well-deserved sleep.

An hour later Alicia was pacing the living area of her suite, her long, ivory silk nightgown swirling around her ankles, the matching silk robe undone and half off her shoulders. Her blond hair, usually swept into a twist, swung loose. She'd scrubbed the makeup from her face and gone through every other nighttime ritual she could think of.

Still she couldn't sleep.

Occasionally muted sounds floated up to her from the party below. Gina had promised her guests quiet, and this evening proved it. It was unlikely that over six hundred guests would be in the lobby at one time again. But the faint party sounds reminded Alicia that Jace Bartholomew was one of the revelers. That thought was keeping her awake.

Jace Bartholomew. The name had a quiet ruggedness that suited the man perfectly. He was a little over six feet tall, forcing Alicia to look up at him. That was unusual, because with spike heels she was almost six feet herself. His shoulders were broad, his waist slim, his hands long and graceful.

But it was his eyes that fascinated her. They were a beautiful blue. Intense, just like the man. But they lacked the vital ingredient that gave a clue to the personality. They showed no emotion. Sometimes he'd allowed laughter, anger or even derision to show. But there'd always been a shield between what he wanted others to see and what he actually felt. Did he feel anything? she wondered.

She was accustomed to reading people. If it were possible to read what he hid, she'd say that Jace Bartholomew was a very unhappy man.

At thirty-six years of age, Alicia hadn't spent her whole life in isolation. She knew that men and women were attracted to each other all the time. If you walked into any bar, you found them dancing around each other in conversation inviting familiarity. But that scene wasn't for her. She ran as far away as she could.

Lately she'd slowed down enough to realize that no one was chasing her, that all her running was done from habit, not of necessity. In the prime of her life, she was now the success she'd set out to be.

And she was still single.

The biological clock was ticking, and suddenly she could hear it. The more she thought about it, the louder the ticktock sounded.

She didn't want a baby right *now*. But time and Mother Nature were taking away her freedom of choice—whether or not to have a child. Her mother had begun menopause at the age of forty-two, just six years older than Alicia was at present.

She plopped into an upholstered chair and swung her long legs over one plush arm. A lot of good it did to have blond hair and long legs. She was single and without options as far as children were concerned.

Indulge yourself and have a fling, a part of her argued. The notion was tempting, also unfamiliar territory; territory as strange to her as the surface of Mars.

"Not on a bet," she muttered. Her life was exactly how she wanted it. She didn't need to look for complications, just to learn to enjoy its peace and serenity.

A knock on her door sent serenity flying out the window.

"Who's there?" Alicia asked.

"It's me, the newest bride-to-be!" Gina called. "Open up before I drop this darn tray!"

Alicia relaxed and did as she was told. "Aren't you supposed to be celebrating your engagement, Ms. O'Con? Soon to be Mrs. Brad Bartholomew?"

"I am," Gina chided with a look that spoke volumes. "With you in your room, since you won't join the party."

Alicia followed her friend into the living-room area and watched as Gina placed a tray laden with champagne and canapés on the low cocktail table. "I was there. I shouted congratulations with the rest of them."

Gina popped the cork from the champagne bottle and poured it into two fluted glasses. "Did you? I couldn't see past Brad." Her look was sheepish yet happy. ·

Alicia laughed. "Is this the tough, no-nonsense businesswoman who told me that Brad only wanted her in his bed?"

"The very same. And I was right." Gina lifted her glass. "I just didn't believe it was for the rest of my life."

Alicia clinked her goblet against her friend's. "To the rest of your life with Brad."

"Hear, hear."

The champagne was chilled to perfection. "Speaking of the devil, where is Brad?"

Slipping off her shoes, Gina took a couch pillow, laid it upon the floor and sat down. "He's in the bar with Jace and Cam. They have a few things to talk over before Jace leaves."

"Oh." Alicia stared into her glass. "Is Jace leaving soon?"

"Immediately. They're taking the family jet and dropping Graham in Dallas. Then Jace is going on to Chicago."

"In the middle of the night?"

Gina sighed. "They all seem to travel at night. They refuse to waste perfectly good business hours by being in the air."

"And is Brad leaving, too?"

Gina's smile grew brighter than a slice of the sun. "Not yet. Brad's moving his corporate offices here so we'll be able to raise our children in the hotel."

Alicia sat back, stunned. "He's doing that for you?"

Gina nodded. Her own expression was slightly dazed. "Isn't that wonderful?"

"Gina, that's terrific!" Alicia congratulated her friend sincerely. "I never really thought that any man would make room for the woman in his life. But Brad just proved me wrong."

"I know what you mean. But it's perfect, really. Since the corporation specializes in constructing or acquiring commercial real estate, they already own a building in the Galleria area, not far from here. And with Graham retiring, the brothers said they didn't care where the offices were. Graham was the only one who wouldn't move from his beloved Dallas."

"I'm awed." Alicia knew she was still grinning. "You've found a rare man, Gina, and no one deserves it more."

"Thanks. I do deserve it, don't I?" her friend said happily. "It's a tough world out there, but you and I have made things possible. You and I have worked together off and on for at least the last four years that I can remember."

"Five," Alicia corrected, studying a cracker with something foreign on it. "We met when you were managing that small hotel in the wine country and I was called in to decorate it, remember?"

"Right," Gina confirmed. "But the point is that we reached success through hard work and thousands of lonely hours piled one on top of the other while everyone else was having a good time. Now it's our turn."

She held out her glass for another toast and Alicia clinked again. "To our turn."

After sipping at her drink, Gina bit into a canapé. "Was I wrong or did I see you and Jace wandering into the bar together?"

"You did." Alicia picked up another cracker and pretended to examine it carefully. "We did."

"And?"

"And what?" Alicia asked, afraid to say anything until she knew where her friend was going with this conversation.

"And what did you talk about? What do you think of him?"

"He asked if I wanted to decorate his building in Chicago. I thought he was one of the rudest and most insensitive men I've ever met." There. She'd said it. Maybe in time she'd mean it.

"Oh, Alicia, I'm so sorry," Gina said. "I guess I'm so darn happy I want everyone to be in love. Or at least in lust," she amended with a chuckle. "Even Brad commented on how great you two looked together."

"Looking great together is hardly a criterion for getting together," Alicia commented dryly, wishing Gina was right and one automatically followed the other. "Besides, he's a mere child." She hadn't given his age any thought when she was with him, but knew he was younger than her.

"Child, my foot," Gina retorted. "Who are you kidding? That guy was *born* old. And as if his childhood with Attila the Hun's mother wasn't enough, he married a true witch of darkness who then taught his daughter to hate him. The man has several damn good reasons for not being on his best behavior with women."

"I've heard the rumors, Gina."

"You just believe that anyone even a month younger than you is out of the running," Gina scoffed. "You're obsessed by your age."

Alicia sipped her drink, not paying any attention to her friend's accusation. She'd heard it before. Nonetheless, Gina's opinion of Jace was the same as her own. He *was* old for his age. In some ways he almost reminded her of an old man, certainly of one past his prime. She hadn't yet figured out why, but she would.

"It doesn't matter," she said and shrugged. "We have nothing in common."

"Darn. And I was hoping you two would hit it off. Brad said . . ." The sentence remained incomplete and Gina looked chagrined. "It doesn't matter. I'm just glad you're here to share the triumph, since you put in so much hard work in making Casa Mañana a success."

"And since this is a triumph, Gina," Alicia added, putting her glass on the table, "I think you ought to join the celebration. No hostess should leave her own party, especially when it's a business celebration."

Reluctantly Gina stood. "You're right, of course. There's at least another hour of revelry to go before I can catch up on my sleep."

"Or whatever," Alicia observed dryly. Brad was staying in town and she doubted it was because *he* needed sleep.

Gina chuckled. "Or whatever," she repeated, leaning over to give her friend a hug. "Meanwhile, catch up on yours. Not that you need it. You're one of the most beautiful women I know."

"As if it matters. That and a dollar will buy a cup of coffee."

"It does matter," Gina declared firmly. "Dress ugly and walk the street and see how you like it. You'll never know how lucky you are unless you find out how the unlucky live."

Alicia couldn't help but chuckle. Gina was forever repeating truisms in her Pollyanna way. But she was right. "I'll remember," Alicia promised, kissing Gina's cheek. "And I'll also remember to call the desk for a wake-up call. I leave at six in the morning."

"I'm not saying goodbye." Gina's smile dimmed slightly. "I'll see you soon, and I'll be talking to you by phone even sooner."

"As usual."

When Gina left, Alicia sat back in her chair and stared at city lights through the gauze-covered window. But her thoughts were elsewhere.

Gina was right. It was about time she was thankful for what she had, and stopped crying over what she didn't have. In some ways she was acting like a child. She didn't want to play with all the toys but didn't want anyone else to, either. Not that she thought of Jace Bartholomew as a toy...

Another knock on the door interrupted her reverie again. This time she opened it with a smile of anticipation. "Gina, I've been doing—"

Jace Bartholomew stood in the doorway. Alicia felt his gaze run up and down her nightgown-clad body like silken fingers. Her breath caught in her throat at the blatant sensuality of his look.

"I'm not Gina," he said finally, as she wrapped her robe more tightly around her. "But I do come bearing gifts." He held up her small evening bag. "Will this do?"

She stared blankly at the purse, then suddenly realized she'd left it on the cocktail table in the bar. "Thank you," she mumbled, reaching for it.

But Jace was quicker and pulled it back out of her reach. "Aren't you going to ask me in?"

She lifted her head, wishing she was wearing heels. Any height would be an advantage. "Aren't you supposed to be leaving for Chicago tonight?"

Jace nodded, his blue eyes never leaving hers. "Yes. But I still have time for some civil conversation."

Alicia smiled sweetly. "I'm sorry, but I don't. Besides, civility isn't a quality I connect with you."

"At least give me a chance to disprove your opinion."

She shook her head. "I'm going to bed now, as you can see."

She saw Jace's brows rise; he glanced over her shoulder toward the sitting area. "Alone, I presume?"

"No," she snapped. "With seven dwarfs."

Once more she saw his beautiful smile. "Were you born with that sharp tongue or was it acquired over the years?"

His smile grew wider, but she refused to answer. Instead she said, "Do you know? You look like a sweet, angelic cherub when you smile. You look like the devil when you don't."

"I *am* an angelic cherub when I smile."

"I get the feeling it's the reverse." Alicia loaded her voice with sarcasm. She held out her hand. "May I have my purse now, Mr. Bartholomew?"

"Are you going to say thank-you?"

"Only after it's in my hot little hands, Mr. Bartholomew." She narrowed her eyes and gave him her haughtiest stare. It usually crippled most men, but seemed to bounce off Jace.

Jace gave a deep, theatrical sigh and placed the purse upon her open palm. "I bet they are hot, too."

A shock of sexual awareness shot through her body. Then she became angry. What right did he have to play sexual word games with her? "From what I understand, word games aren't your usual style. Why change your mode of operating now?"

Jace leaned against the doorjamb, totally relaxed. He crossed his arms over his chest, accenting the strength of his arms even through his suit jacket. "You're right, they're not. But for some reason, when I'm around you all sorts of things I don't usually think about come to mind. It's as amazing to me as it is to you."

He looked like a cross between one sexy hunk of a man and a precocious little boy, and Alicia couldn't help the smile that she felt tugging at her lips. "Do you think that if we ever meet again, you could try to rein in your tendency to blurt out sexual innuendos?"

"Oh, we'll meet again," Jace promised, smiling in return. She was mesmerized. "I'll try to be good." He raised one hand in the air. "I promise."

Alicia nodded, accepting his word for it. "Thank you for returning my purse. I hope you have a pleasant trip home."

"Thank you," he responded as formally as she had. "And I wish you the same."

He straightened and gave her a light salute. "Until next time."

Alicia didn't answer. If she had her way, there would be no next time.

With a look that was intended to speak volumes, she gently closed the door, then walked directly into the bedroom, flicking off light switches as she went. Sleep was her only hope to stop herself reviewing their conversation over and over again—and fantasizing that there had been more to their discussion than there really was.

Reaching the bedroom, where a mirror ran the entire length of one wall, she turned on the bedside lamp. She stared at herself with detachment. Gina was right. She was beautiful. She was also thirty-six years old— older than the man who had just stood at her door tossing out sexual teasers.

"Enough, Alicia. He's younger, you're out of your league and you know it." She didn't know how much younger he was, but certainly younger than Brad, who in turn was younger than herself. Right now everyone seemed younger.

Her mirrored self seemed to agree, and she turned away.

Flicking out the light, Alicia lay down on her back and stared at the ceiling. She was doing exactly what she had promised herself not to do. She was repeating her conversation with Jace in her head.

Well, she was leaving bright and early in the morning and would probably not have an opportunity to see Jace again. They moved in separate circles—and in separate cities.

Thank goodness!

2

THE TRIP HOME to San Francisco was uneventful. Alicia sat in first class, busying herself with the inevitable paperwork that multiplied with every job. An older man seated next to her tried to start up a flirtation, but her chilly, blank stare halted him in midsentence.

It was noon by the time she caught a cab and reached her Victorian combination home and office just outside Mill Valley. Last night's hotel opening and Jace Bartholomew's probing comments had taken a toll on her nerves. As today was Sunday and there was nothing of immediate importance she needed to do, she took a warm shower, curled up in bed and fell sound asleep.

Darkness had descended by the time Alicia abruptly awoke, startled by the jarring ring of the telephone.

"Alicia?" Jace's tone was low and soft, with just a hint of a Texas accent. She felt the deep vibrations of his voice all the way down to her toes. They curled in response, but her sleep-fogged brain was too vulnerable to fend off the reaction. Her body hummed to the caressing sounds of his voice before she could steel herself against him.

"Yes?" She hoped she sounded haughty and disinterested. And prayed he'd believe she didn't recognize his voice.

"How was your trip home?"

"Who is this?" That would put him in his place.

"Jace Bartholomew." Was there a hint of laughter in his voice? She couldn't tell but had a sneaking suspicion there was.

"What can I do for you, Mr. Bartholomew?" She glanced at her alarm clock. It was nine at night in San Francisco, which made it eleven in Chicago.

"I'm sending you some information on the Bartholomew Building. I want you to view it with an open mind."

Her emotions seesawed back and forth between wanting to listen to his voice all night and wishing he'd hang up and leave her alone. She didn't know which she wanted more.

Every word evoked a vivid mental image. His piercing blue-eyed gaze. His broad shoulders fitting snugly into a perfectly tailored suit. The masculine scent of his skin. His rudeness. "I'm always open to new business," she hedged. "However, I'm busy for the rest of the year. I told you that."

"And your secretary told me otherwise."

"My secretary was wrong," Alicia told him for the second time. Talking to her new employee would be the first item on her long list of things to do in the morning.

"So you said." His voice lost that teasing quality and she missed it, but not enough to tempt fate by giving him what he wanted. She wasn't even sure what that was, but wasn't ready to find out, either. Jace talked about his building, but the underlying tension between them wasn't business. She was experienced enough to recognize that. It was sexual. And if sex was what he was after, it wasn't available. No sense in tempting fate.

"Is there anything else, Mr. Bartholomew?" Her tone was as crisp as she could make it.

"Jace." Now it was his turn to snap and Alicia felt a twist of satisfaction. She wasn't the only one reacting strangely. "And I'll talk to you again after you get the information."

"I'm not interested, *Mr. Bartholomew.*" She refused to use his first name. "But thank you for calling. I'm flattered to learn the Bartholomew Corporation thinks so highly of me."

"Obviously not flattered enough to change your mind."

"Business is business," she retorted brightly. "And I'm in the middle of it right now. So if you'll excuse me . . ."

His chuckle was as low and sensuous as his voice. "Good night, Alicia," Jace said softly, apparently not at all bothered by her turndown.

"Good night, Mr. Bartholomew," she replied firmly and clicked the receiver into its cradle.

There. She'd done it. She'd probably turned down the plum career opportunity of the year. But she'd also escaped being tempted by the wrong man. For reasons she didn't logically understand, she knew that Jace Bartholomew had at the very least the power to confuse her. At the most he could hurt her.

She wasn't masochistic enough to put herself through that.

Plumping up the pillows, Alicia leaned back against the headboard. According to the mirrored closet doors opposite, a frown was considering making a permanent home between her delicately arched brows.

Why was Jace able to throw her off balance so easily?

Most of her business associates were males. She
worked well with them. There had been only one occasion when she had tried to turn the business relationship into a more personal one and it had not been
a wise choice.

The owner of a drugstore chain had wooed her with
flowers and candy in dimly lighted restaurants featur-
ing succulent finger foods. He'd been rakish, charming
and had almost swept her off her feet. She'd really been
tempted. Then she'd found out there was a Mrs. Drugstore Chain Owner who was always available to pick
him up and cuddle him after each of his little flings. And
Alicia had learned that the age difference between Mr.
Drugstore and his wife was over ten years—she being
the elder. She also held the purse strings. Looking back
now and recalling the little things he'd said made Alicia believe his wife had tightened those strings from
time to time.

No. Alicia knew she had made the right choice by
putting Jace out of her life and her business. She might
occasionally be lonely, but was also sure of the direction her life was taking. Experience had taught her that
man trouble always came nicely wrapped. So did Jace,
and that was part of what made her wary of getting any
closer. Right now she called the shots and decided what
she needed. No one else.

JACE SCOWLED at the phone as though it were respon-
sible for Alicia's turndown of his magnanimous offer.
In all fairness to the instrument, he hadn't succeeded
when he'd asked her in person, either.

He glanced at the file in front of him, wondering if it
would do any good to tempt her with the dozens of in-

terior photographs of the building, along with the architect's rendering, then rejected the idea.

Damn.

Maybe he should forget about hiring Alicia to decorate and try to recruit his architect's second choice. After all, the world was full of decorators. The project could win the successful candidate the cover of *Architectural Digest*.

So why was he so disappointed?

He honestly didn't know.

She'd done one hell of a job with Gina's hotel. Alicia had also done superior work in other hotels and office buildings. In her early days, while she was still struggling to establish herself, his father had seen her spark of genius and hired her for properties he owned in California. Alicia's ability to create a practical workplace while making it warm and inviting perfectly suited what Jace envisioned for his building.

The problem was her inability to see him as anyone other than the obnoxious man in the bar. He couldn't understand what had come over him that night. He'd goaded and teased her into leaving his company, only to follow and continue his harassment.

She brought out the worst in him, and still he wanted more time with her. He was crazy!

Rubbing his temples, Jace leaned back and closed his eyes. It had been a long day and an even longer evening. Admitting that his phone call to Alicia was the highlight of his evening told him how desperate he was for diversion. He should have lined up a date for this evening. Then he wouldn't be sitting here alone, wondering what to do with himself. He could have forgotten his troubles in the arms of another woman. At least for a few hours.

He sighed. Some people called him a woman-hater, but that was only a small part of the truth—he didn't trust women. He always left a woman before she became an encumbrance. He'd learned at an early age, first through his mother and then his wife and daughter, that most women were only out for themselves. When a woman said "I love you," it meant she wanted something. Leave-It-to-Beaver's mother wasn't real. She was a figment of some writer's twisted and deranged mind. He ought to know, for he had desperately looked for that elusive woman often enough in his childhood.

Well, he could do without the opposite sex in his personal life. He wasn't stupid enough to believe that chasing rainbows led a guy to a pot of gold. All he'd ever gotten for his trouble was manual labor, digging in the wrong spots to find nothing but more dirt.

No woman was worth the effort it took to create even a bad relationship.

That told him he wasn't after Alicia's tall, slim body. He wasn't trying to woo her into letting him run his fingers through her silky blond hair. His fingers didn't really itch to stroke the pale translucence of her skin. He didn't care that her legs were long and supple or that she walked with the grace of a sleek, sensuous cat. None of that mattered.

He only wanted her to take the job. Was that so much to ask?

She turned you down twice. Why are you still trying? a little voice asked.

He had no answer.

With a heavy sigh, Jace picked up the file and slipped it into a UPS envelope. Tomorrow he would have it shipped to Alicia's office and see what happened.

All she could do was say no. Again.

ALICIA'S HANDS shook slightly as she opened the envelope. Jace Bartholomew had sent it overnight from his office and she knew it was more bait. He was still trying to hook her.

She was right. Photographs spilled over the surface of her desk.

There were about thirty of them. Each caught the old building in its best—and worst—light. The photos revealed the building was in dire need of a decorator. They also showed the wonderful possibilities for turning the Bartholomew Building into a showcase.

Intricate plasterwork on the ceiling cried out for restoration, not destruction. The floors, now covered in brown industrial carpet, were probably either of stone or oak. As if to hide the interesting design, dark brown file cabinets were shoved into nooks and crannies carved out of the walls. Roller blinds set in the window frames looked like hundreds of deep-set closed eyes.

The photos highlighted flaws, yet those same flaws were the building's greatest potential assets.

She stared at the last shot before picking it up. A piece of paper floated from its back and landed on her desk. A message from Jace.

What do you think?

Jace

Alicia smiled grimly. If he had included even a hint of a personal message, she would have tossed the whole mess into another envelope and sent it back to him by express mail. Instead she was intrigued.

"Damn you, Jace Bartholomew," she muttered, staring at the note. "You've offered a challenge. But though I can't see the strings attached, I know they're there." She leaned back. "Somewhere."

Shifting through the pile again, she caught sight of a few other intriguing little details. Tall and narrow recessed windows that reminded her of a church marched around two sides of the lobby. A marble floor in the same area wrapped up the wall. If the photo was accurate, it was a polished gray, finished in an old technique that was no longer used because of its cost. Only true craftsmen could do the job well, even in the building's heyday. And this work seemed to have been done beautifully.

Then some idiot of a decorator had stretched dark, characterless paneling from the marble baseboards to the twenty-four-foot ceiling. Awful.

The alarm system downstairs hummed, then turned off. Her new secretary had arrived for work. "Hi," Joy trilled, taking off her raincoat and hanging it on the rack near the door. "How was your trip?"

"Fine," Alicia answered. "And how was it here?"

"Oh, great. I learned the old customers' names and who goes with what file. That took over a week." She laughed, sitting down in the chair opposite Alicia's desk. "I thought I was back in school again, memorizing names and dates and all the stuff."

Alicia grinned. Joy was only twenty-two. School wasn't that far behind her. Then she remembered the talk she needed to have with her new secretary and felt her smile slip. "And did I receive any emergency phone calls I don't know about?"

"Yes," Joy answered promptly, reaching for a file. She pulled out five or six pink telephone slips and handed them to her boss. "And then I forwarded two or three to the hotel."

Alicia raised her brows in question. "Who?"

"That project in Albany, New York, needed your okay immediately. Didn't you talk to them?"

"No. They never called." Alicia felt anger building, but held her tongue. Joy was new to the world of business and Alicia knew she had taken a chance when she hired her. She couldn't get too angry when she hadn't explained all the ground rules. But she wasn't sure how much common sense Joy had.

"When did that happen?" she asked, then looked down to see it recorded on the message. Nine days ago. By now they had probably taken her lack of answer for an answer. No.

"Then Jace Bartholomew called and asked to reach you immediately. I told him you were in Houston dealing with a hotel opening."

"Did he say what he wanted?"

Joy nodded her head energetically. "He said you were to decorate the Bartholomew Building in Chicago, but he had to up the beginning date to immediately. I told him I didn't think that would be a problem, since you had set aside the next few months for a job in Albany and they seemed to think you didn't want to do it."

Alicia took a deep breath. "Joy," she began, trying to keep her temper under control, "if the president calls and asks us to redecorate Air Force One, you don't tell him what my plans are. Instead you reassure him that I will get in touch with his office immediately. Then, if you can't contact me, you instantly call my private answering machine and leave a message to that effect. Do you understand?"

Joy leaned forward. "Yes, but—"

Alicia cut her short. "There's no reason good enough to tell someone where I am or what my work schedule is," she stated firmly.

"Yes, but—"

"Especially a businessman you haven't met and never filed a contract for."

"Yes, but—" Joy stopped, as if expecting Alicia to interrupt again.

Alicia sat back and waited.

"But he said that he had a deadline," the girl ended lamely, apparently realizing how weak her excuse was. "I shouldn't have done it."

Alicia smiled. "Right."

Joy's eyes widened. "My God! He could have been a pervert out to get you! It could have been dangerous!"

"Right."

"I won't do it again," Joy promised, suddenly subdued.

"Okay, I believe you. But remember, even if Jace Bartholomew promises you the moon, you don't tell him where I am or volunteer my business plans."

Joy crossed her heart with one pink-tipped finger. "I promise."

"And that goes for anyone else. Right?"

"Right." Joy leaned forward again. "But tell me. Did you meet him?"

"Yes."

"And, uh, did his looks match that sexy voice of his?"

Alicia pursed her lips, then grinned. Joy was a young girl with a young girl's dreams. Even Alicia had to admit she'd been a little shaken by that voice.

"Yes," she acknowledged. "However, he's still a potential client. Good looks and a sexy voice aren't reason enough to spill information about my business."

"I gotcha," Joy retreated to her own desk. "And from now on I'll be Mata Hari, seeking information but never giving it."

"Somehow I don't think your analogy is right," Alicia stated dryly. "But I think I get your point."

It was time to catch up with business.

The first day back in her office set the pace for the rest of the week. Alicia finished the necessary paperwork for Gina's hotel, assured suppliers that checks were in the mail and ordered samples from fabric and wallpaper wholesalers. Paying bills took up all of one day. At night she did laundry and grocery shopping and sent out dry cleaning.

But throughout the long days and busy nights, Jace's photographs were always on her mind. Sometimes she even found them in her hand. The project was a truly wonderful challenge, and her emotions continued to seesaw back and forth.

She knew that if it weren't for her mixed feelings for Jace, she'd take the job in a New York minute. Jace was the stumbling block. He shook her equilibrium and made her think of personal opportunities she might have chosen to reach a more fulfilling life.

Things like marriage, family and little babies that smelled sweet and smiled like cherubs.

Alicia didn't want to think those thoughts. Not now. She'd already wrestled with those imaginary demons and believed she'd won the battle, made the choices. She couldn't change that now, only go forward with her life from here. The ticking of a biological clock shouldn't make her change a decision taken with logic and forethought.

The long trip to Houston and back had tired her out.
After all, Gina's hotel hadn't been an easy assignment.
Everything that could have gone wrong had.

Jace made her feel vulnerable. She didn't know why.
He was exactly the type of man she usually stayed away
from. Then there was his age. In her mental book of
rules that was a no-no. Then there was his attitude toward women in general and to her in particular.

His approach to her had been cruel. No finesse.

No wonder she was confused!

She was reacting to a man who sent mixed signals.
He either admired her business acumen while overlooking her obvious femininity or liked her business
acumen and thought he could browbeat her because she
was female.

She couldn't make up her mind.

Alicia was still struggling with the problem when
Gina called from Houston, sounding very happy as she
rattled off her wedding plans.

But it was her request that startled Alicia. "And that's
why I'm calling," Gina told her friend, finally catching
her breath. "I want you to be my maid of honor."

"Of all the people you could have picked, why me?"
Alicia asked. "Won't you hurt someone's feelings?"

"No." Gina's voice was firm. "You were there in my
toughest times. You gave me your expertise, advice and
a shoulder to cry on. Please say you'll do it."

"I'll do it," Alicia said obediently. "When and where
am I supposed to be?"

"The ceremony will take place a week from Saturday in front of the hotel's water wall." Gina laughed.
"I tried to talk Brad into a church wedding, but he said
I was from heaven and the water wall is from the earth,
and that's enough of a cathedral for him. What could I

do? The water wall was his idea, anyway," she added indulgently.

Gina was obviously willing to humor the man to almost any degree. And Alicia knew it wasn't a one-way street. Brad indulged Gina, too.

"Who's the best man?"

"Jace, of course." Hardly able to contain her happiness, Gina chuckled again. "But Cam will be there, too."

Alicia tried not to let her heartbeat quicken enough to change the tone of her voice. "I would have thought it would be Graham," she finally managed to say.

"Graham said he would rather watch than have to remember to participate. When he retired, he *really* retired."

"Well, he's sweet, anyway," Alicia said.

"Sweet as a recently fed viper," Gina commented dryly. "He's always been kind to me, but I've seen the business side of him. He's a man with a purpose. And heaven forbid if his purpose crosses yours."

"Well, he's retired, so half your troubles are over."

"Right. Now my husband-to-be holds the mortgage papers on *my* hotel. This ought to be an interesting relationship. At least our pillow talk won't put us to sleep."

This time Alicia laughed with her. Brad was much like his Uncle Graham. They both had definite ideas and followed them through. Brad's best-defined concept to date was that, come hell or high water, Gina was his. And he'd pursued that goal with amazing single-mindedness. Now there was true love between them, the kind that had surpassed all the hardships they'd had to go through during a courtship that had so often been made difficult by Gina's future mother-in-law. Mrs.

Bartholomew's behavior seemed to have affected each of her three sons very differently, Alicia reflected.

After the two agreed that one of her favorite cocktail dresses would be good enough to use as a bridesmaid's dress, Alicia promised Gina she would be in Houston the day before the wedding to help make sure all the arrangements were in order. They both knew there would be nothing for her to do but give moral support, because Gina, ever organized, would have things under control. Hanging up the phone, Alicia leaned back and contemplated her friend's good fortune.

Even in the darkness of Gina's initial rejection, Brad had never given up hope. That was love, all right; the kind that books and songs were written about.

Alicia had never experienced that kind of love. Probably because she'd never allowed herself to be in a position where she would have to choose between a personal and a business life. Gina was lucky; her love story had a happy ending that many women would never achieve. Alicia still felt herself too vulnerable, unable to overcome the disappointment of a love gone wrong. To be sure, now that she was older and wiser she knew that what she had felt in college had been puppy love and hurt pride. It had helped protect her from falling in love again, but that was okay. Better never to love at all than to go through the heartbreak of losing the one you loved.

That thought led to another.

Jace Bartholomew.

Unlike his brothers, Brad, who was willing to put his feelings on the line for the woman he loved, or Cam, who loved every woman too much to love just one, Jace was reputed to be a woman-hater. He had no respect for women. In fact he'd been blunt, forward and rude with

Alicia. And she was still drawn to him. That, more than anything, told her she shouldn't be around him for any length of time.

But Jace will be at the wedding.

It didn't matter. She'd ignore him and return home as quickly as possible. Maybe she'd get away from everything and take a vacation. She hadn't had a vacation in years. Ixtapa in Mexico would be the perfect place to relax. Instantly she felt better for having decided on a course of action. A smile curved her lips. Certainly her secretary could handle the office and forward any important calls. Especially since their little talk.

And she could display the fine art of the "cut direct," as they used to say in Regency novels, whenever she saw Jace. That would put the man in his place. Sooner or later he would have to admit that for Alicia he was the wrong man.

Pleased with herself, she reached for the phone to make the reservations. Before she changed her mind....

JACE STARED at the phone, willing it to ring. Alicia must have been tempted by those photos. She had to have thought long and hard about the challenge—the project of a lifetime. She'd have to be insane to turn this plum down.

Not insane, just wary of you, his conscience told him. He'd blown it. He'd been too blunt, too brutal. And she had retreated. He'd never seen any woman back off so quickly. He'd love to know the story behind her reaction.

He grinned. Gina would know.

But getting information from Gina would have to be done in person, when her defenses were down. She'd never satisfy his curiosity over the phone. She protected her friend.

Jace leaned forward and pushed the phone buttons that automatically connected him with the New York office and his brother Cam.

Finally Cam was on the line. Jace got right to the point.

"Listen, little brother, I need your help."

"What kind of help?"

"I need a dossier on Alicia."

"Alicia, the decorator?" Cam whistled. "You don't fool around, do you?"

"I don't have time." Jace didn't add that he didn't have the resources for this job, either. Cam was the head of the security department for Bartholomew Corporation.

"Why do you want information? You know she decorated Gina's Casa Mañana Hotel. What else do you need to know?"

"I want personal references. I'm thinking of using her for the renovation in Chicago."

Cam muttered an expletive. "I don't believe you, big brother," he scoffed, "so you can cut out the bull. If you wanted references, you'd ask Brad or Graham. You want something else entirely. You want personal. Why?"

"Look, just do as I ask." Jace should have known better than to go through Cam. Cam believed that every time a man looked at a woman it was the beginning of the world's most passionate romance.

"All right, all right." Now Cam was trying to placate him. "But I want to know why you need it. You're not telling me half the story."

"You'll be the first to know," Jace lied. "Meanwhile I'll fax you the particulars. You can have your men dig from there."

Jace hoped Cam had enough love interest in his own life without hearing about his brother's. But apparently that wasn't the case. "Right," Cam confirmed in a sarcastic tone. "I'll get back to you in a few days."

"Good enough." Jace decided it was time to change the subject. "Are you flying into Houston directly for the wedding or coming here first?"

"I'm going direct," Cam answered. "I'm bringing a friend with me. Tell Brad to get me a nice room, will you?"

The friend was a woman; Jace would stake his reputation on that. Cam was the direct opposite of him. Drawn to the opposite sex and loving none exclusively, he loved them all.

Jace chuckled. "Brad said to make our reservations through the front desk, just like everybody else. It doesn't matter that he's marrying the hotel owner. He's got her too busy to bother with his pesky brothers."

Cam's laughter filled the phone. "He doesn't have time to bother with *anybody,* let alone family. He's too busy making one for himself."

"Isn't it about time you did the same, little brother?" Jace teased.

"I will when you do, big brother," Cam retorted dryly. "And we all know the chances of that, don't we?"

Still smiling, Jace ended their conversation. At least Cam and he agreed on two things. Neither of them would every marry. Unlike Brad, they weren't ready to settle down. And both thought Brad wanted a family almost as much as he wanted the job of CEO of the Bartholomew Corporation. That possessive gleam in

Brad's eyes told him Brad would never lose his love for
Gina. Brad had always had a soft spot for her. They'd
known each other since their teens. But only when Brad
had returned to Houston to confront his father had he
fallen in love with Gina, the daughter of his father's
mistress, and fought to gain her love. Amazing.

Jace wished he could have experienced that kind of
love just once. Now, at thirty-two, he felt too old for
that sort of unending passion.

Certainly he had never experienced it with his wife.
Maybe that was why he'd felt so shattered when she'd
asked for a divorce. He'd always felt guilty for not being
madly in love with her, and had worked harder than
he'd ever worked at anything to make her happy. He'd
done all the right things, making sure they had time
alone, sending flowers and candy on the appropriate
occasions and asking what she did with her days.
Nothing had worked. As the years passed, she'd become more resistant, more demanding. She'd turned
into a full-fledged shrew, though he was never certain
if it was because that was her nature or because she'd
realized he would never love her the way she wanted to
be loved. He could forgive her for that. But when she'd
lied about him and turned their daughter against him,
that had been the last straw. He just didn't trust women.

Both Cam and Brad had tried to tell him he was
wrong about women, but he wasn't buying it. Every
woman he'd gone out with since his divorce had displayed similar characteristics.

That was what made his attraction to Alicia so odd.
He didn't understand the fascination. She certainly
wasn't the usual type he was tempted by. Maybe he just
needed a good lay, and his hormones had chosen her.

That wasn't right, either.

He had an idea she might be older than him, but that wasn't worth more than a passing thought. Who gave a damn? She certainly knew more of the workings of the business world. She had an instinct that had been honed sharp. That was stimulating. Of course, he also wanted to take her to bed, to make mad, passionate love to her all night long. He wanted to run his fingers through her blond hair and touch her creamy, almost translucent skin.

But it was more than that. She was a woman he wouldn't mind waking up next to afterward. In fact, he was sure he'd enjoy it and wanted the opportunity to find out. There was just one small problem. Because of his behavior in Houston, she was now running scared.

Going against his gut feeling, he dialed her number anyway. When she answered, he took a deep breath. Her voice flowed smoothly, like liquid honey.

"Have you had enough time to think about the Chicago project?" he asked in a more brusque tone than he'd intended. He softened it. "It's perfect for you. You know that."

"Who's the architect?" she asked, and he was startled by her directness.

"Ambrose, Tyler and Anderson," he answered, unable to stop satisfaction from lacing his voice. They were one of the top firms in the country. It was just another tidbit to bait the hook.

"Lucky you," she replied dryly, but Jace had the feeling she was impressed.

"Thank you."

"And when is this project to start?"

She was still asking questions. That was a good sign. "The architect has completed his planning. Now he needs to know who the decorator will be."

"Who's their choice?"

"It doesn't matter. I want you."

"Thank you, Mr. Bartholomew. But I'm afraid I'm not available. I'm leaving for a well-deserved vacation immediately after the wedding."

"Cancel it."

"No can do. It's paid for and I'm not in the habit of throwing money around." Now it was her turn to sound satisfied.

That made his temper rise. He took a deep breath, unwilling to rush her with his rudeness again. "How long is your vacation?"

She hesitated before answering. "A week."

"And then?"

She hesitated again, and he knew he had her thinking quickly. Good, that was usually when people made mistakes. "Then I'm doing a building in Albany."

"Albany doesn't deserve you. I do."

"I'll think about it," she finally hedged. Then he knew she wanted to decorate his building.

He grinned. "Okay, Alicia. Think about it while you're gone. The photos aren't lying. The building is a professional challenge and you know it."

"I know it," she repeated softly.

"See you in Houston," Jace promised. Then he hung up.

His grin turned to laughter. *The lady says no, but she wants to say yes.* If it took him all week, he'd make her say yes to this deal. Then he'd see what else he could make her say yes to.

He pushed the Call button on his phone. Seconds later his secretary stood at the door.

"Virginia, cancel my appointments for the week after Brad's wedding."

"Going somewhere?" She didn't look at him. Instead she peered through her bifocals as she jotted down a note or two on her ever-present steno pad.

"I'm taking a vacation."

That got her attention. Bright blue eyes stared at him, surprise plainly written across her face. "Where to?"

He chuckled as he imagined Alicia's expression when she learned what he'd done. "Damned if I know. I'll give you that information right after Brad's wedding."

The middle-aged woman looked concerned. "Are you feeling okay?"

"I'm feeling great," he reassured her, still smiling broadly.

Virginia tried to be businesslike most of the time, but Jace knew her mother-hen instincts came to the fore on odd occasions. She was obviously still not convinced of the state of his health, but at least knew when to back off. "If you say so, boss. I'm just a little surprised. You've never taken a vacation before."

"Then it's about time I did. You always tell me I work too hard."

"Yes, but you enjoy the hectic pace."

"Well, now I'm going to try doing what other men do—take time off."

She shrugged, but kept her eyes on him. "Maybe this is the right time to take a rest," she finally agreed. "For the past few days you've been acting like the giant who's ready to fricassee Jack."

He laughed again, but this time aimed the laughter at himself. She was right. He hadn't been the most pleasant man to be around lately. "You're not the only one who's surprised," he admitted. "But I deserve some time off." *And it's the one move Alicia won't expect,* he thought smugly.

A vacation was the perfect answer.

3

HOUSTON WAS BUSTLING, as usual. It was a wonderful town to work in, but the pace exhausted her, Alicia decided as she leaned back to enjoy the ride to the hotel, refusing to think about anything other than the wedding and her business. She would not think of . . .

Shifting in the leather seat, she stared at the Houston skyline as the cab whisked down Interstate 45 toward town. With no traffic and a good cabby, she'd be at Gina's hotel in less than half an hour.

The image of Jace invaded her mind. She tried to block it, but it returned again and again. His smile was haunting. He could look both young and old, playful, yet weary of playing games. And her own emotions were just as confused. She wanted to either slap his face or hold him close.

Darn the man!

The cabby pulled off the main street and into the curving driveway, halting only when he reached the side of the hotel doorman. Alicia's artistic eye scanned the exterior. It was perfect. She relaxed as the door was opened and the uniformed man held out his hand to help her from the car.

"Welcome to Casa Mañana, Ms. Dumont," he murmured. Then he nodded his head toward a bellhop as the driver opened the trunk and took out her luggage.

"Thank you. Do I know you?" she asked.

"No, ma'am, but your picture is on Miss O'Con's wall. And everybody knows the name of the decorator who did this place," he said, his smile broadening.

"Well, thank you for taking the time to notice," she answered and entered the hotel. The large lobby, divided into smaller conversation areas, felt crowded. Business was plainly booming.

She got into line at the desk, but the bellboy tapped her arm. "I have your key, Ms. Dumont."

"Who checked me in?" she asked, surprised.

"Miss O'Con has been waiting for you. You're in the suite next to hers," the young boy answered. He led her toward the elevators, which looked as if they floated, once freed from their base in the center of the rectangular lobby.

She was ushered to the top floor of the hotel and into a lovely suite. It was the first one she'd designed. The hotel living quarters were across the hall with only one other suite on this, the VIP floor.

A chilled bottle of award-winning Texas wine had already been decanted and was sitting in a silver bucket on the low coffee table. Alongside it was a basket of fresh fruit. Delightfully mixed spider mums and daisies graced a clear crystal bowl on the desk.

The staff had done a wonderful job. If Alicia's reception was any indication, this was going to be the "in" place for those who demanded luxury and craved privacy.

When the chimes rang, telling her that someone was outside her door, she smiled with satisfaction at the muted, melodic sound. She had chosen well.

Her smile faded when she opened the door.

Jace leaned against the jamb, hands in his pockets as he surveyed her just as hard as she did him.

"Did you have a good trip?" he asked, and his words poured over her like a honeyed caress.

"A very good one," she confirmed, determined not to let him know just how much he affected her. She refused to ask him how his trip had gone. She didn't want to get involved. "Is there something I can do for you?"

It was a bad choice of words. He stared deep into her eyes until she was forced to look down. That was a mistake, too. Worn jeans clung to strong legs and lean hips. They had almost faded to white where they conformed to his masculine curves. She tore her eyes away with difficulty.

His blue-eyed gaze strayed past her. "May I come in? I'm not too fond of discussing anything in hallways."

She had no choice. He was to be the best man at her best friend's wedding. Alicia was also certain that his suite was next to her own. There was no sense in being rude and letting him know how he affected her. He'd guess in a minute what she was covering up. Emotions. Thoughts. An irresistible sexual pull toward him.

Alicia stood aside. "Please do."

His walk was almost a stroll as he entered the living area and went straight to the decanted wine. Holding up the bottle, he silently asked if she would join him in a glass.

She gave a nod and primly sat down on the couch, watching him fill two glasses. He handed one to her, then, still standing, raised his glass. "To a better future."

She stared at him. "Was the past so bad?" It was a challenge to discuss whatever had made him bitter.

Jace chose to dodge the issue. "Terrible, but I'm willing to forget it, if you are."

Alicia couldn't keep the sarcasm out of her voice. "My, is that an apology, Mr. Bartholomew?"

"Jace." It was a demand.

She nodded, acknowledging that it was silly to keep up the formality, but remained wary.

He smiled and the creases on each side of his mouth deepened. He looked even sexier, if that was possible. "Yes, it is an apology. I never should have—" he hesitated "—I never should have chosen the words I did when I spoke to you in the bar. It was unnecessary."

"And callous."

He nodded in agreement. "And callous. But I couldn't seem to get a rise out of you and I wanted to know what would happen if you were hit below the belt."

She tilted her head. "Why?"

Jace shrugged, then took a sip of his wine. "I wanted to know how you handled it."

She had a feeling he was hedging on his answer, but she didn't know for sure. "Have you tried this on other unsuspecting people?"

"A few," he admitted. Jace moved around the table and sat down at the opposite end of the couch. The cushion moved slightly and Alicia tensed. Even with a foot or two between them, he was too close. He leaned one arm along the back of the sofa and she sat up straight. Alicia knew he saw her move but couldn't help it. If she had remained where she was, his hand would have touched her shoulder....

"Is there a problem, Alicia?" He was taunting her again, his voice much lower than before.

This was her room, and she wasn't about to leave, so her only recourse was attack. "Trying a new technique? Insults didn't work, so now you're moving in for a seduction scene?"

His blue eyes narrowed. The room fairly hummed with tension. "I told you I was sorry about the insults. It was a mistake, one I'm not too proud of."

Alicia clasped the wineglass so tightly that her fingers turned white. "I don't know what you came in here for or what you want. I'm not sure I want to know. You and I have to make the best of this situation while we're here. I don't want anything to detract from Gina's big day. Her wedding is important to me."

He leaned closer, almost taking her breath away. "And then?"

"And then we can both go our separate ways and forget apologies and awkward moments," she said softly, her attention fastened on his mouth. He had a full bottom lip that cried out to be nibbled on. That startled her. She'd *never* thought that way before!

"No." His voice was equally soft. "We begin to work on a relationship. Together."

She barely had enough strength to repeat the word. "No."

His head dipped still closer and she was forced to look into his eyes. "You really are beautiful." The words were a caress.

"No." She wasn't answering his comment, but still thinking of the word "together."

"We'll have the next few days to see how well we get along."

"No."

"Then we'll decide if we each go our separate ways."

She gave in. His eyes were mesmerizing. "All right."

Her heart pounded in her ears. With a slowness that was sheer torture, she watched his eyes blur as his mouth came close enough to touch. Her eyelids drooped and she caught her breath.

The meeting of their mouths was a long awaited pleasure, yet not nearly enough. His parted lips grazed hers, then touched again. The contact was just a promise of what was to come. He brushed her bottom lip, before perhaps giving in to temptation, and lingered to taste its sweetness.

Alicia was growing dizzy from the lack of air. Her thoughts couldn't separate action from emotion. She was dazed, caught by his very touch in a tenacious web. His tongue dipped to taste her lips more fully and she caught her breath again, then uttered a light sigh.

She didn't move. She couldn't. Jace pulled back and looked down at her. Her lashes were barely open but she could see the desire deep in his blue eyes.

Alicia found herself leaning toward him, wanting—needing—more. He obliged her by stroking her lips into submission once more before finally crushing his mouth upon hers.

His hands curled into her hair, closing around her face, holding her still as he explored the moist softness of her mouth. A moan echoed in the room and she wasn't sure if it came from her or Jace. She didn't care as long as he continued to kiss her. Her own hands crept up to curl around his neck. Her palms felt the pounding of his pulse against her skin and she reveled in the knowledge that he was as shaken as she.

When he pulled away again, Jace leaned his forehead upon hers, letting his warm breath mingle with hers as he tried to catch his breath and slow the beating of his heart.

She allowed her hands to drift back into her lap. Reason returned slowly but inexorably. He had to know she'd wanted more. She had all but begged him to take command and go further.

"You are more potent than the best champagne," he finally said.

"So are you."

He pulled back. There was a crinkle of laugh lines around his eyes that Alicia found endearing. "We're quite a combination," he teased softly.

She answered him with a shaky chuckle.

"We should do that more often," he went on.

She cleared her throat, wishing she could clear her head as easily. "Why?"

"It beats fighting any day."

Fighting. This was Jace Bartholomew she'd been kissing as if she longed to be in bed with him. This was the man who hated women, the man she had decided to stay away from. Now she knew why. He was the most potent male she'd ever encountered.

Alicia pulled away and reached for her glass of wine. "I wasn't the one who started fighting. You were."

"And now I've stopped."

She couldn't look at him. "So it seems." She sipped the cool liquid and wondered where the flavor had gone. But the taste of Jace's kiss still lingered enticingly on her tongue.

He sighed. "I didn't mean to bring up anything unpleasant."

"Don't worry. I've had to deal with unpleasantness before," she stated, her tone bitter. Why was she attracted to a man who not only hated women but seemed to think she was fair bait?

"I want peace between us, Alicia." His tone was so sincere that she looked up at him involuntarily.

"What kind of peace?" she asked, caught yet again by his gaze.

"The kind that allows us to be civil to one another, so we can be together in the same room and not tense up with the expectation of a fight. The kind that allows us to relax in each other's company."

"And that was behind the kiss?"

He nodded.

"I see," she said, trying not to show her disappointment. She should have seen that coming. From any other man she would have suspected an ulterior motive. But her radar wasn't working very well. In fact, she was sure it wasn't working at all! At least Jace had admitted that his kisses had been a modern form of the peace pipe. He'd wanted peace, so he'd gone right after it. She remembered her father's motto: *Do whatever it takes to get the job done.* That was what Jace had done. So why did she feel so deflated?

She tried to smile, but felt the muscles surrounding her mouth pinch with tension. "Let's try it," she prompted. "Only the next time we meet, we don't have to kiss to break the ice. A smile will do."

His blue-eyed gaze grew even more intense. "Will it?" he asked. "I liked my way better. It takes the chill off the day."

And turns on the heat. But she was obviously the only one who had a problem recuperating from a simple kiss. Her heartbeat was still erratic, her pulse staccato.

He smiled, slowly this time. Her pulse reacted by increasing its tempo. "Can we declare a peace, Alicia?"

She nodded, swallowed, then answered. "Of course."

"Good." He reached for his glass of wine, then clinked it against her own. "To a new friendship."

"A new friendship," she echoed, her mind still swirling. A friendship with Jace Bartholomew? *It would never work!*

Jace finished his wine with a giant swallow and stood. "Thank you for the opportunity to apologize," he murmured, staring down at her.

"You're welcome."

A moment later he was gone. She could breathe again. At least their antagonistic relationship was over. So why did she have the unsettling feeling that Jace had won...?

JACE LAY DOWN on his bed and let out the air he seemed to have been holding for the past half hour. His mind was still whirling with the feelings that kissing Alicia had set in motion.

His hands still shook from touching the soft, fine strands of her hair. His lips continued to taste her. His body persisted in wanting her. He rubbed his palms against the comforter beneath him, wishing Alicia were lying beside him, naked.

Thought you wanted her for her expertise, Bartholomew? Expertise in what? He knew it wasn't sex. She seemed to be as new at that as a baby lamb willingly led to the slaughter gate. When he'd brushed her lips, her reaction had been painfully easy to read. He hadn't gone any further for that reason. He couldn't let her hate her reaction to him—or her own actions—when she had time to think.

Her response had been a mirror of his own. It was hard to believe that in this cynical day and age he could respond so quickly and strongly to a simple kiss. But he had. And he still wanted her.

This was crazy! No one had ever before made him ache so quickly. It had to be a fluke. He wasn't just reacting to *Alicia*. In his present frame of mind he might have reacted the same to any beautiful woman. He was alone too much.

With that thought he rose, washed his face and hands and headed downstairs to the bar, where he would wait for Cam to arrive. Maybe a drink would quench the thirst for overindulging in the intoxication that was Alicia.

WHEN ALICIA walked into the bar, she spotted Cam, Jace and Brad immediately. She began to turn to head back out again, then heard Brad call her name.

"Alicia, over here."

Unless she wanted to be rude, there was no way out. Pasting a smile onto her lips, she pivoted and walked to their table. Brad rose and gave her a hug and a kiss on the cheek. "I'm so glad you came. Gina and I wouldn't feel complete if you weren't with us."

She had to laugh. "Complete? Who are you kidding? Half the time you two didn't know I was around!"

"But the other half of the time we were glad you were there," he told her with a sheepish grin on his handsome face. Now that he had Gina, he could admit how much in love he was, Alicia reflected. And his expression was one of relaxed contentment, which seemed to bear this out.

"Speaking of the other half, where's Gina?"

He chuckled ruefully. "She's on the phone, demanding more flowers for the wedding." Brad pulled out a chair and motioned for her to sit next to him.

Without glancing at Jace she did so. Brad signaled to the cocktail waitress and she came over to take Alicia's order of gin and tonic.

"Doesn't that taste like quinine?" Jace asked innocently when the drink appeared.

"Yes," she answered, stirring ice cubes and trying to match his teasing tone. "But occasionally I need a good dose of it to keep away malaria—and a few other diseases."

Brad and Cam looked startled. "Malaria?" Brad asked quizzically. "I thought they'd found a cure for that?"

"Well, for most strains," she conceded. "But there are one or two left that still need an occasional treatment." She lifted her glass and silently saluted Jace. If she was going to be forced into his company, she might as well have a little fun with it.

Jace's glance was appreciative, and she had a feeling he knew exactly what she was thinking—and approved. It was a heady thought. It was also a little scary.

Just then Gina came in, a tiny bundle of barely leashed energy. "Alicia!" she exclaimed, giving her a hug and a kiss on the cheek. "I had every intention of running right to you but I got sidetracked by the wedding details. I'm so sorry, but one of the bellhops told me that Jace visited you, so I knew you weren't completely alone!"

At the mention of Jace, Alicia flushed. A glance in his direction told her he was uncomfortable, too, and she saw three other pairs of eyes swing around to stare at him.

"A welcoming committee of one," Cam declared, a smile on his face. "That's my brother."

"My, my," said Brad. "Isn't that considerate." He sipped his drink, then looked innocently at Cam. "He's an inspiration to us all, isn't he, little brother?"

"Certainly is," Cam agreed blandly. "But what can I say? Everything I know I learned from my brothers. This is just another example of good upbringing."

"All right, guys," Gina told them firmly. "Cut it out. You don't need to embarrass Alicia any more than she already is." She turned to her friend. "I'm sorry, Alicia. I should have known better than to say anything in front of these clowns."

Jace was as angry as Alicia was embarrassed. "I should have known that you two weren't old enough to be allowed out without a keeper. But your time will come, brothers. And it won't be a pretty sight."

Both Cam and Brad apologized to Alicia and she accepted. It was a relief, however, when the subject was dropped without further investigation.

They made plans for dinner and chatted until Alicia finished her drink. Then she rose. "Thanks for the drink, but I have some work to do if I'm going to get to take my vacation."

"Where are you going?" Gina asked.

"Ixtapa, Mexico."

Jace stared up at her, his blue eyes pinning her where she stood. "When?"

"Next week."

"When next week?" he persisted.

"Monday," she answered reluctantly.

She saw a smug expression flit over his face. "I know you'll have a good time."

Alicia nodded distantly. "I'm sure I will." She pushed in her chair. "See you later," she called as she left the dim confines of the bar and headed toward the elevators.

She dressed for dinner carefully, knowing she'd be only inches away from Jace. An extra spray of perfume helped boost her confidence. When she had finished, she stared into the mirror, seeing a beautiful, competent woman who looked as if she was filled with self-confidence. She wished the inside matched the outside. Usually it did. Only when Jace was around did her insides turn to mush.

To bolster her courage, she gave herself a confident wink, picked up her purse and strode toward the door. It was business as usual, Alicia reminded herself. And she held that thought until she was halfway down to the lobby. At that point she glanced at the terrazzo floor below and spotted Jace watching the elevator descend. He was wearing a dark suit that must have been custom-made because it fitted his body perfectly.

The butterflies took up residence in her stomach again.

"You look beautiful," he said as the doors glided open and she stepped out.

"Thank you." She knew there was a sparkle in her eyes that he'd put there, but couldn't help it. Her gaze took in his broad shoulders and trim hips. He had shaved recently and the light tang of his after-shave was tantalizing. If it was possible, his blue eyes looked even bluer. She was surprised to note the gleam in his eyes. Was that a hint of personal interest? Normally his expression gave nothing away.

Jace crooked his arm. "May I escort you to dinner?"

She smiled, recklessly deciding to thoroughly enjoy the rest of the weekend—and Jace's company. After Sunday she'd probably never see him again. "You may,"

she said lightly, accepting his offer and his arm. "Lead
on."

Jace did. Gina, Brad, Cam and Graham sat at a long
table toward the back of the restaurant. Their greeting
was effusive and Alicia felt the warmth of belonging to
a group. It was a nice feeling. Like family.

She was seated directly across from Jace, between
Brad and Cam. Gina, her eyes twinkling with happiness, was sitting next to Jace.

With much ceremony, the waiter uncorked the
champagne and poured. Brad was the first to raise his
glass. "We're celebrating two important occasions tonight," he announced. "Not only am I marrying the
most wonderful woman in the world, but this restaurant has just been given a four-star rating." He looked
lovingly at Gina. For a fleeting moment Alicia was
jealous of their relationship. "And if my future wife has
anything to say about it, I'm sure by our first anniver-
sary it will be rated a five-star restaurant, a most cov-
eted prize, but no challenge at all for Gina O'Con, soon
to be Bartholomew."

Everyone added their own personal congratulations
to the festivities, then Graham Bartholomew stood up
and harrumphed them into silence. "To Gina and Brad.
She's the only woman whose mettle is as strong as mine,
and that means that she and my nephew are well
matched. May they have a long and prosperous life."
His portly stomach jumped as if he could barely hide
his laughter. "And give me many grandnephews and
nieces to dote upon."

Alicia stared straight ahead, afraid to look at anyone for fear they would see what was hidden in her
heart. *Children.* Gina, her best friend, would have
children to dote upon, love, care for. And Alicia would

not. Like a toothache, it was a constant dull pain that had been a part of her so long she was used to it—almost.

Automatically Alicia picked up her glass. But when she looked across the table, Jace's knowing eyes were watching her.

It was a good thing he couldn't really read her mind.

4

DINNER WAS DELICIOUS. Every once in a while Alicia glanced up to find Jace's gaze still on her. Why was he smiling like that?

More toasts were celebrated, more wine flowed, more food arrived. Cam's brothers teased him for having arrived alone. His explanation that he wanted to be with his family rather than the tall, long-legged redhead he'd been squiring—and for whom he had booked, then canceled a room—was met with boos and jeers. Alicia had heard the rumors of his "girl outside of every business meeting" life-style. Although she enjoyed talking to Cam, she was also leery of him. He reminded her too much of her youth—when she had believed that love could overcome any obstacle.

The wedding rehearsal didn't get underway until almost midnight. Although the group had been laughing and joking until then, it grew solemn as Alicia and Jace exchanged places with the bride and groom and walked through the marriage ceremony. Alicia could tell Gina and Brad both wished this was the real thing. They were plainly so in love and so caring with each other that she had to blink back tears; after all, she didn't want to make a fool of herself.

Jace leaned forward and whispered into her ear. "You might as well cry at this one, Alicia. They'll never be as happy as they are right now."

"They're making a commitment for life, not for a five-year renewable contract." Even though she whispered, her voice was firm.

Jace shrugged his broad shoulders and stared at the couple. "No one knows, including them."

"You're a cynic."

"Yes. And you must be, too, or you would have married by now."

"You mean because I'm still single?" She positively bristled at the comment. It was a sore point. How dare he make remarks like that!

"Just so. If you're over twenty and believe in marriage, why haven't you joined that wonderful institution?"

"Because men aren't all they pretend to be," she snapped.

"Neither are women, Alicia," he drawled. "You ought to see your fair sex from my vantage point. It would be enlightening."

"It's a slanted view, and certainly not based on reality."

"How would you know?"

She gave him a frosty smile. "I'm older. Didn't I tell you?"

"Wisdom doesn't necessarily come with age." His eyes searched her face. "And apparently age doesn't always show."

She ignored that observation. "Wisdom doesn't necessarily come with gender, either."

Alicia saw heads turn at his deep chuckle. The smile he gave her was one of admiration—and pure enjoyment of their exchange of wit.

"Can I offer you a drink after this is over?" he asked, his warm breath caressing her cheek as he leaned toward her.

The idea was too tantalizing. She shook her head. "No, thank you. I've got to get some sleep."

"Alone?"

"Don't ask me that again," she told him. "It's none of your business."

"You're right," he conceded. "But the type of man you would choose to spend the night with interests me." He stared down at her until she wanted to squirm, but she refused to give him that satisfaction. "What would he be like?"

Alicia turned and stared straight ahead, pretending she was listening to the directions the rotund minister was repeating for the tenth time.

"Cat got your tongue?"

"Are your manners so hard to remember?" she countered through gritted teeth.

Jace chuckled again. Again all eyes turned toward them. This time Alicia could feel the blush that she was sure tinted her cheeks a brilliant pink.

Then the rehearsal was over. With Gina at his side, Brad shook hands with the minister while Graham beamed. But before Alicia could leave the company of the family, Cam strolled over to her.

"What could you be discussing that would make Jace laugh so much?" Cam asked, hands in his pockets as he surveyed her.

"I wasn't talking at all. You'll have to ask your brother what spurred his laughter."

Jace intervened. "I'm not talking, little brother. I don't give information out about those I'm involved with."

Once more Alicia bristled and she turned to do combat with the man.

But one look at the definite twinkle in his eyes, at the smile he wore so beautifully, and she was a goner. Anger dissipated, warring tension seeped away, and suddenly she was laughing with him.

Cam watched in amazement. His brother, who never smiled, was laughing with Alicia, who never smiled. A miracle.

Jace cleared his throat, but the merriment was still in his eyes. "May I walk you to your door?"

"Are you going to behave like a gentleman?" she questioned.

He raised his fingers in a Boy Scout salute. "I promise I'll try to remember my manners."

Cam stared at Jace, astonished. "What happened to 'Bah-humbug where women are concerned'? What happened to 'All the world's a commode and some damn woman has her hand on the handle'?"

Jace didn't bother looking in Cam's direction. His eyes were fastened on Alicia as his hand drew hers through his crooked arm. "Say good-night, Cam."

"Good night, Cam," his younger brother dutifully repeated. But it was too late. Jace and Alicia were gone.

"ARE YOU ALWAYS so quick to bite back?" Jace asked as the elevator began its ascent.

"As quick as you are." She waved at Gina below. Until this minute she hadn't realized that Gina didn't know they'd left.

"And as defensive?"

She turned, leaning against the inside railing as she examined him. "Again, I'm only as defensive as you are."

He cocked his head and his dark hair shone in the muted lighting, revealing highlights she hadn't noticed before. "Why?"

"I have my reasons, Mr. Bartholomew. As I'm sure you have yours."

"Mine are on record for the world to know. I have an ex-wife who would make Godzilla look like a house-trained monkey." He stared at her. "But you were never married."

She nodded. "We all have episodes in our life we'd rather not talk about, but which influence us just the same."

"And you won't tell me yours?"

She shook her head, her attention still captive. The small space hummed with expectations, hopes, dreams and memories of disaster. Alicia wasn't sure which emotion was winning. All she knew was that her heartbeat feathered against her ribs in a rhythm that was way too erratic.

When the doors opened, Jace stood aside to allow her to exit first. She walked ahead of him, but her pace was slow. She didn't want the quiet, relaxing time between them to end, but was so tired she could barely keep her eyes open.

When they reached her door, Jace held out his hand and she slipped the key into his palm. Each leaned against one side of the jamb; apparently neither was willing to end the night, she thought.

Alicia spoke the first words that came to mind. "Gina's pregnant."

Jace's eyes widened, he seemed to consider the thought, then nodded in agreement. "Yes."

"Do you think Brad knows?"

Jace thought again. "No. I think Gina's going to keep her secret for a little while longer."

Alicia's curiosity was aroused. Jace obviously knew his brothers well and was willing to talk about them. "Will the prospective father be happy about it?"

"Happier than I'd be." Jace's mouth turned down in a grimace. "Ignorance is bliss."

Alicia saw hurt in his eyes. "You have a daughter, don't you?"

He stiffened. "Yes."

She couldn't keep herself from prodding. "Don't you like children?"

His expression closed. "No."

"Not even your own?"

"That's not up for discussion."

Clearly she'd touched a very sensitive nerve. Since he'd done that to her, she had an idea how he felt. Alicia slowly nodded her head. "Fair enough."

He looked at her sharply. "Is that it?"

"What?"

"Is that all you're going to say?"

"It's obviously a subject you don't want to discuss, so why pursue it?"

He reached out a hand and gently twirled a strand of golden hair around his finger, touching the soft skin of her neck as he did so. His full mouth turned upward into a teasing smile. "Why, indeed?" he murmured.

Her body hummed once more. The hotel corridor light cast a shadow onto one side of his face, creating a study in contrasts. On the side that captured light he was handsome and very vulnerable. But the dark side was bitter, almost sinister.

Curtailing her fanciful thoughts, she cleared her throat. "Are you going to unlock my door?"

He narrowed his eyes. How slim her neck was! He watched the rise and fall of her breasts and stilled his hand. "Are you ready?"

She read his signal. He was asking more than if she was ready to go inside. He wanted to join her. "For a good night's sleep. Alone."

His hand fell and her neck felt chilly without the warmth it had imparted. With a smooth, deft movement he unlocked the door.

Angry with herself for feeling dejected, she crossed the threshold. Before she'd taken two steps, he called her.

Her name was barely a breath. "Alicia?"

Against her will, she turned to face him. They stared at each other, tension arching between them. For a long moment it was all Alicia could do to remain where she was. She wanted to walk into the comfort of his embrace, wanted to rest her head upon his chest and feel his arms curl around her.

Instead she stood very still, afraid to move and transform thought into deed.

Jace closed the space between them. His gaze locked with hers, he placed both hands upon her slim shoulders.

Her heart felt locked in her throat.

He leaned forward and placed a very chaste, very soft kiss upon her forehead.

"Sleep well, Alicia."

And then he was gone. The door closed quietly behind him.

Alicia remained where she was. Every muscle in her body was taut. Uttering a long sigh, she finally allowed her breath to escape into the warmth of the air where Jace had stood just seconds before.

Why hadn't he kissed her as he had earlier? Why had he kissed her at all? Was that the kind of kiss a man would give his mother or sister? The idea hurt more than she wanted to admit, even to herself. Had he wanted more intimacy, as his words had suggested, or was his veiled advance a figment of her imagination?

She had no answers.

Sighing again, Alicia turned and walked into her bedroom, flipping out lights as she went. Once in the bathroom she faced the mirror and stared into the hazel eyes that stared back at her. "You're one confused lady, Alicia Dumont."

DRESSED IN nothing but a pair of black bikini Jockeys, Jace paced the living area of his suite, too uptight to go to sleep.

Every time he closed his eyes, Alicia was there. Smiling, laughing, saddened, angry; she was there all the time.

She was one intelligent and intuitive lady. She had known Gina was pregnant when no one else knew. Looking back, he realized all the signs were there. Gina had been smiling secretly for weeks. More than once he'd seen her holding her stomach as if pleased about something.

He knew Brad would be thrilled. His brother had always wanted a family. In many ways Cam had the same dreams. Even though he went through women at an alarming rate, it was because he was searching for something that he hadn't yet found. Jace was sure that when the right woman came along, Cam would stay with her forever.

Jace knew he was the odd man out. At one time he'd thought family life was what he wanted, too. He'd been wrong. His marriage had been a disaster. Then when his daughter, Meagan, was born, he had once again dared to hope he could have a real family. That had been a mistake. He'd been granted close to three years of bliss with Meagan before his wife had begun to limit the amount of time he could spend with the child. Any and every pretext had been good enough—a trip, visiting grandparents. Only after the divorce had Jace realized she'd been trying to get even with him. And in a way she had. By the time the divorce was finalized, Meagan had become a whining, demanding child who connected his every visit to the presents he brought. At first he'd gone along with it. Guilt was a great impetus for spending money to alleviate its symptoms, yet it had never worked. Meagan had continued to whine, money to flow, and his ex-wife had gone on harping.

After two long and painful years, Jace had admitted defeat and bowed out of their lives. Instead of going through the wringer of rejection by his daughter and barely leashed anger from his ex-wife, he now mailed a healthy check once a month. They could do what they liked with it, but they could no longer take a strip off his hide at every visit.

But the fond memories of Meagan lingered. Every once in a while he tested them like a child testing a loose tooth. They were still there, still active, and he was still reluctant to part with them....

Barefoot, Jace strode to the bar, fixed a glass of Perrier with a fresh twist of lime and gulped it down.

Alicia had not pursued her questions about Meagan. Odd. He'd never before known a woman capable of dropping a subject. He had said "No discussion," and she had honored his wish. Amazing. Even he couldn't do that. At least not on the topic of her love life. Questions about the type of man she was interested in ate at him constantly.

He'd asked Cam to look into it for him, but so far Cam hadn't said anything. Perhaps it was time to give him a boot in the rear and remind him.

As if on command, Cam's key card jiggled in the lock. The door opened and he stepped in, pocketing the card as he approached his brother.

"Is this the alternative to finding a woman?" he asked dryly, taking in the drink in Jace's hand.

Jace answered automatically. "This is better."

"Like hell." Cam shrugged out of his jacket and threw it over the nearest chair. With a tug he loosened his tie and undid the top two buttons of his shirt. "What you're doing isn't even a substitute for boredom."

"Speaking of boredom," Jace observed, pouring the remainder of the bottled water into his glass, "I wish I had some reading material."

Cam poured himself a small shot of scotch. "Are you hinting about the report on Alicia?"

"Yes."

"It's in my briefcase, brother. But if you're looking for stimulating reading material, you can forget it. That woman has led one boring life." He shook his head in mock regret. "I can't see why. Aside from her beauty and intelligence, she has the magic to make a woman-hating ogre laugh."

"Don't make fun of a relative!" Jace called over his shoulder as he headed for Cam's briefcase.

"At least you recognize yourself."

With the file in his hand, Jace stretched out on the couch and began reading.

"Say thank-you, Cam," his younger brother muttered.

"Thank you, Cam."

Jace skimmed the report, looking for clues. Then he saw it. An engagement announcement from the *Los Angeles Times*. Alicia had been planning to marry a law-school student. But no wedding had taken place. Instead, upon graduation, she had gone to work for an interior design firm in New York, and her boyfriend had married another woman. The report revealed that he'd become a father within three months of the wedding. Was that the reason the wedding had been called off? Had the man had a wandering eye?

He searched for some mention of other men in her life, but there was none. She'd been seen with certain businessmen at various parties, but none were rated steady boyfriends.

Interesting.

She was an only child raised by highly motivated parents. No cousins. Her father had died when she was fifteen, while her mother had fallen ill and died in Alicia's sophomore year.

No wonder she was a loner.

"Interesting reading?" Cam asked, strolling to the side of the couch and looking down on his brother. He took a sip of his drink. "It seems to me that she's led a rather dull life."

Jace snapped the file shut. "Compared to you, Romeo, everyone leads a dull life."

"Maybe," Cam conceded. "But Alicia's personal life has been more than dull. It's the next-best thing to death."

Jace laughed. "Isn't that the truth! And I'm about to spice it up."

He saw Cam look at him searchingly. Jace stood and stretched, a smile still on his face. "Is another Bartholomew brother about to succumb to the charms of matrimony?" Cam inquired.

"Not this one," Jace countered, transforming his smile into a determined frown. "I'm just intrigued with the idea of showing a beautiful, successful woman that there is more to life than work."

"If that isn't the pot calling the kettle black, I don't know what is." Cam gulped down the rest of his drink. "Besides, I like Alicia. You hurt her and I might get angry."

Jace raised his brows. "Since when did you get so protective of the female sex?"

"Since my brother the barracuda decided to go swimming in a pool full of innocents. I might be a womanizer, but you, Jace, are a woman-hater. That's far more dangerous—and harmful."

"Call it quits. I don't want to harm Alicia. I just want to show her a good time. She'll enjoy it, I promise you."

"And how are you going to do that when she leaves tomorrow?"

Jace knew his expression was smug, but couldn't help it. "I'm leaving with her."

ALICIA PREPARED for the wedding with special care. She refused to believe the reason was Jace. She just wanted to look extra special for Gina's Big Day, she kept telling herself. But she knew better.

She had dreamed again and again that Jace had kissed her the way she wanted to be kissed. Again and again she had woken up, unwilling to complete that dream. But her body's reaction had told her it was quite willing to continue with the fantasy.

The dress she'd chosen for the wedding was a mint-green silk sheath that flatteringly stopped at midcalf.

Shoes with three-inch heels matched the outfit. Alicia pulled her hair into a Gibson-Girl knot. She stood back and eyed herself critically. The effect was exactly what she wanted.

"Your looks haven't gone yet," she muttered to the image in satisfaction. She picked up her matching bag and walked out the door.

Large silk screens artfully divided off the water wall portion of the lobby from the rest, so that normal hotel traffic wouldn't interrupt the proceedings. Alicia stepped off the elevator and walked directly to the small crowd gathered by the wall. Jace, Cam and Brad stood to one side with the minister. Alicia had to smile. She didn't think she'd ever seen Brad look as nervous as he did right now.

Without another glance in their direction, she went to Gina's office; she knew her friend would be just as nervous as Brad.

She was right.

"I knew I should have had the big mirror brought down," Gina mumbled from her perch atop a desk chair, trying to catch a glimpse of herself in the mirror on the wall.

"Are you trying to kill yourself or just do bodily harm?" Alicia asked.

"Thank goodness you're here!" Gina exclaimed, making the chair do a precarious dive. "Do I look all right? Is my dress the right length? Can you check my makeup?"

Alicia was only able to answer when Gina ran out of breath. "You look beautiful, and your dress is perfect," she confirmed.

Gina's smile was tinged with relief as she stepped from the chair to the more secure floor. "Thanks. Is everyone out there? Did you see Brad?"

"Everyone except Brad is waiting patiently for the bride. He looks very handsome—and very nervous," Alicia said on a laugh.

A gleam appeared in Gina's eyes. "Really? Good. I was ready to elope, but he was the one who wanted this ceremony. He can sweat it out."

"Right," Alicia murmured. "Does that mean you want to stay in here indefinitely and let him continue sweating? Or would you rather put him out of his misery now?"

Gina tilted her head, appearing to give the question deliberate consideration before smiling. "Let's go," she said, and Alicia knew she was as eager as Brad for them to become husband and wife.

Alicia walked down the aisle first, with Gina following. She stood to the left of the bride, while Jace stood next to Brad. The religious ceremony was short but beautifully worded.

Alicia listened to the exchange of vows and wanted to cry. She would probably never have a husband or the family she craved. Of course she knew she could have a child without a husband, but what she really wanted was a *family*. Being a single parent was not in her plans.

The service drew to a close and everyone gathered to congratulate the groom and express their best wishes to the bride. Alicia knew Jace was standing just behind her and imagined how his soft breath would feel on her neck. The restaurant staff and a few of the personnel who worked behind the desk stood at the back. Just before the group broke up, they clapped in honor of their boss and her new husband.

The reception was small, private and beautiful. Flowers were everywhere, in tall vases on the floor, on the table in arrangements, on the wall in woven baskets. Alicia mingled, purposely paying no attention to Jace. He hadn't spoken to her, either. In fact, after chasing her for the past two days, it was strangely deflating not to have him talk to her, although when she glanced up, she caught him looking at her with a friendly smile. But still he stayed away. She refused to admit that she missed his attentions.

So much for feeling sultry, sensuous and dangerous.

By late afternoon Alicia had said her goodbyes to everyone, including Gina and Brad, had packed her bag and hailed the limo to the airport.

It was time to forget about Jace, work and biological clocks. This was her vacation—time to think about nothing.

She stepped into the lobby of the intercontinental airport and went directly to the gate. After receiving a boarding pass, Alicia stepped onto the plane and found her first-class seat.

She stopped before she sat down. Her mouth flew open, her eyes widening as she stared at her seat partner.

"You're blocking the aisle, Alicia," Jace said softly. "Why don't you sit down and let the people pass?"

She did as she was told. She couldn't think of anything else.

5

SHE KNEW she should be angry, but joy got in the way. So she buckled her seat belt and sat back to enjoy the ride. After all, this was her vacation.

The plane taxied down the runway and took off. When the stewardess came around with coffee and juice and champagne, Alicia flipped down her tray and asked for champagne. Jace ordered a Bloody Mary. She knew by his changing expression that he was upset about something. Funny. She'd only known him two weeks and already knew how to read him.

She smiled.

Jace sighed, resignation tinging his voice as he spoke. "Aren't you going to ask me what I'm doing here?"

"No," she said, sipping at her drink. "I think you already know what you're doing."

"But *you* don't."

Her brows rose. "I assume you're traveling to Ixtapa. Isn't that this flight's destination?"

He grinned, and her heart tripped. "Smarty."

"Yes." The lightheartedness that she had lost during the wedding returned. She had a week off and Jace was with her. What more could she ask? "How long are you staying?"

Jace crossed his arms and leaned back. His blue eyes twinkled as he gazed at her. "Who wants to know?"

"I do."

"You can't assume the obvious?" he drawled.

"With you, Jace, there is no obvious."

"Thank goodness." He leaned back with a complacent look and said nothing else. Now that she had questions, he was obviously feeling better. Like a little boy, the man wanted to be in control. He didn't care for it when the experience was reversed.

A smiling stewardess served breakfast, along with freshly brewed coffee. Despite the fact that Alicia knew she'd get an answer sooner or later, the longer Jace took to respond to her question, the more impatient she became. Was he going to be with her for a week or just a few days? She *refused* to ask again. He could rot before she questioned him further.

The flight was a quick two hours. They discussed books, movies and plays. Alicia was impressed with his reading list, to say nothing of the plays he'd obviously enjoyed. Either he wasn't quite the woman-user the gossip mill had called him, or he at least treated his dates to an evening of good entertainment before shredding them with his rapier tongue. And his knowledge of the background of both authors and music intrigued her. Jace Bartholomew was a very complex man.

"For someone so young, you have eclectic tastes," she finally admitted.

His eyes narrowed and he glared dangerously. "Don't start the age bit, Alicia. It means nothing and you know it. You just use it as a block to keep others away."

"Only younger others," she qualified.

"You're a very opinionated woman, and your logic leaves a lot to be desired. Didn't you know? Women should marry younger men since they have a longer life span than men."

Alicia calmly buttered her roll. "Is that a proposal? If so, I'm sorry, but I'm not the marrying kind."

His tone of voice didn't give away the frustration she hoped he was feeling. "This is *not* a proposal. I'll never do that again." His expression lightened. "Although I might turn it into a proposition if I thought I'd get anywhere."

Her pulse beat faster. Her fingertips tingled with the image his words evoked. They would stretch out on a wide, king-size bed, the percale-soft sheets rumpled and pushed to the bottom. . . . "But that's an impossibility," she stated crisply.

"I agree," he answered calmly. "So can't we be friends without your hang-ups getting in the way?"

"I don't have hang-ups!" she snapped.

"Then what's this age thing? Gina's your friend and she's younger than I am."

"Gina's different."

"She's a friend. Or do you discriminate between males and females?"

"I don't discriminate!" Alicia snapped again, unable to stop herself. She hated to admit it, but he was right. She'd been acting as if they were potential lovers without a future instead of friends with much in common.

"I beg your pardon?" he asked blandly.

Her smile was sheepish, she knew. "All right, so I occasionally make an error in judgment. I'm sorry. Can we be friends?"

He held out his hand, accepting hers. "I thought we already were."

"We were—we are," she stammered.

"Good." He still held her hand, letting his thumb dance lightly across the top and bringing every nerve to life. "Where are you staying?"

"At the Pierre Gardens."

"What a coincidence! So am I."

She looked at him sharply. "And when did you make these plans?"

"Thursday. As soon as I heard you say that you were taking a vacation."

"Why?"

"Because I wanted to be with you."

"And talk me into decorating your building?"

He nodded, clearly unabashed. "Yes."

Alicia relaxed. As long as his pursuit of her was for business reasons she could. "You're willing to take the time for a vacation, even when you know I won't change my mind?"

"Yes."

"You're a gambler, Mr. Bartholomew. But that's your problem, not mine. I'm here for a holiday and I'm damn well going to enjoy it. You can do whatever you want."

"I agree, but thanks for your permission." His tone was dry and she felt a blush crawl up her cheeks.

She refused to give him the satisfaction of another answer.

The plane banked, giving them a view of Ixtapa, then they landed. The blue Pacific rolled toward the shore as if waving a welcome. Alicia's excitement grew even as new questions popped into her head. She'd always loved this part of Mexico, and this time Jace was with her.

By the time they reached the hotel, she was filled with anticipation and a sense of restlessness. Jace insisted she check in first, and she did, not willing to admit that she didn't want to leave him. She determinedly took the elevator to her room alone. After the bellboy had deposited her suitcase, she tipped him and closed the door upon the world.

Alicia walked to the patio. Although it was only the middle of the day, above the pale blue horizon sat a chunky, full moon like a small, wispy cloud. No wonder the waves looked so high.

The ocean tide wasn't the only thing affected by the moon, Alicia thought wistfully, quite willing to blame her own reactions to Jace on the very same phenomenon.

Impulsively she stripped off her dress and undergarments and slipped into her new bathing suit. A royal-blue one-piece with a low-cut bodice and French-style, high-cut thighs, it was quite daring. Glancing into the mirror, she decided the effect was worth what it had cost.

Within minutes she was out of the room and on the beach. Dropping her towel onto a vacant chair, she dashed into the freezing water. It felt wonderful! Alicia dived beneath unusually calm waters and began swimming toward the horizon. Winded, she rolled onto her back and floated, the sandy bottom just below her. Like a shelf it continued far out to sea, she recalled, dropping off when you least expected it. Here the water would barely cover her shoulders if she stood.

She wanted to laugh with the joy of being alive that permeated every fibre of her being. Instead she smiled.

"A mermaid with a sense of humor." Jace's voice startled her and she jerked into an upright position, coming knee to knee and breast to chest with him.

He grinned. "I would have knocked, but . . ." He shrugged his broad shoulders.

"You could have shouted a hello," she grumbled, sensing nonetheless that her delight at seeing him was shining in her eyes.

His hands reached out and spanned her waist, helping her to float even closer. "I could have, but then I would have startled you, too."

"I can swim," she pointed out. It wasn't a protest. In fact, she wasn't about to lose touch with him. Her hands rested on his shoulders, enjoying the tautness of his skin under her fingertips. The motion of the water pushed her up with a gentle wave, then down again, her toes touching bottom just long enough for her to regain her balance before she was swept up again.

"So can I."

Her thigh brushed his and she wondered at the sudden heat of the water. But instead of pushing away, as she had told herself to do, she remained in Jace's grasp, her gaze locked with his until she let her eyes wander, taking note of his strong cheekbones and jawline, then dwelling on his corded neck and broad shoulders. Drops of water magnified by sunlight clung possessively to his dark-haired chest. And beneath the surface of the crystal-clear water she saw black . . .

"Trunks," he said. Startled, her eyes flew back to his. "What?"

"No Speedos, just plain black trunks. Not half as sexy as your suit, but then I bought them two minutes ago from the hotel gift shop. It was either this or a G-string."

She chuckled. "You planned a vacation and didn't pack a suit?"

"I planned a vacation and forgot to pack my suit," he corrected, tightening the grip of his fingers around her waist. One hand splayed across the small of her back, teasing every nerve into awareness just as he had on the plane.

"Obviously you don't go on vacation often."

"Not often enough."

"I thought so. It was either that or swimming in the buff," she teased, breathless at his nearness.

"I wouldn't have minded going naked, except that I didn't think you'd let me this close to you."

Alicia had a sudden sinking feeling. She was on a roller-coaster ride and loving every delicious—frightening—moment. "You're right. Besides, there are other people on the beach."

"Very few." He smiled and she could have sworn he was kin to a tiger. "There won't be any down here tonight," he suggested.

"You don't know that."

"We'll see." He pulled her even closer and she felt the cloth of his suit stroke her thigh. Then his hips bumped against hers and she was melting.

"We fit together. Don't you think?" His voice was low.

She didn't answer. She couldn't. When Jace drew her still closer, she didn't protest, preferring to rest her head against his shoulder and close her eyes.

He was sweeping away any arguments she might have used, but she didn't care. He was taking over, and though she was loath to admit it, that was exactly what she wanted. No decisions to make, no action to take. Just follow his lead and let her emotions take over.

The ocean wrapped them together in one intensely sensuous package. His skin smelled of slick salt water and man and heat and sun. She breathed deeply. The roar of the surf was a distant, lulling sound. In Jace's arms she felt safe . . . and alive.

Jace closed his eyes, all too aware of the water tempting him to press even closer as it wandered intimately around their bodies. With each deep pull of the tide, she swayed toward him, touched, then was gently drawn away. His leg moved between hers, aching to shift nearer, yet he was afraid that if he attempted it, she'd be frightened off. It was torture to hold her like this, it would be worse to have her leave his arms.

Wisps of blond hair teased his back and shoulders, waving gently against his skin like silken seaweed. He held his breath as Alicia's hands stroked him.

"Mmm." The sound came from her throat and reverberated through him, heightening his own awareness.

Ever so lightly, he kissed one temple. "Comfortable?"

She nodded her head, clearly unwilling to lose the contact.

He smiled ruefully. He needed her in his bed soon or he'd be a raving maniac. He couldn't remember the last time he'd responded to a woman as he did to Alicia. Sixteen? Seventeen? Certainly not since, so he was afraid that if he wasn't careful, he'd lose her.

A wave bulged, letting them ride to the crest, then gently dropping them in its wake. When it did so, Alicia's lower body swayed against Jace.

Damn.

Her head rocketed off his shoulder, her eyes darting to his.

"I won't apologize. It's a normal response to having a beautiful woman in my arms."

"I'm sorry, I didn't mean—" she stammered. "I certainly didn't—I never meant to do that."

"I didn't think you did." His voice sounded rough even to his own ears. His breath seemed to be forced out of his lungs as he stared down at the sensuous blond nymph in his arms. "But you did."

She stared up at him, confusion and sensuality in her eyes.

"I want you."

"So you think."

"I know. And I want you now."

Her eyes widened in shock. "Here?"

"Here," he whispered hoarsely. Then his mouth covered hers in a kiss that was as necessary and explosive as life itself. She tasted too sweet, was too tantalizing to lose. His arms tightened around her, pulling her closer than the water could sway them. He wasn't going to give her a chance to say no, not even to think about it. If she didn't want him to make love to her, she would tell him in other ways. But a small voice in his head prayed that she wanted him just half as much as he craved her.

With hands that shook, he slipped the bathing-suit straps from her shoulders, soothing the heated flesh.

"So smooth," he murmured, dragging his mouth away from the softness of her lips to capture the moist warmth of her neck.

Her breathing was light, her breasts moving rapidly up and down as the straps slid lower. Through the clear water he could see their pink aureoles and couldn't resist. Clasping her slim waist, he raised her until he could take one pouting bud into his mouth. Her moan was carried out to sea on a breeze as he took first one, then the other, teasing her, scraping her full breasts with his teeth until her hands held his head and she wrapped her legs around him.

"Jace!" she protested. "There are people!"

"Who can't see a damn thing," he assured her. "We wouldn't be doing this if I thought I'd embarrass you."

"But . . ." she began. Her protest was lost as his lips descended again upon one aching nipple. Even she couldn't remember what her next argument would have been.

Wanting still more of her, Jace raised his head to crush Alicia's breasts against his naked skin and leaned forward to taste her. But when his lips claimed hers, he wasn't satisfied with just a taste. Need raced through his body, compelling him to arch himself against her in primitive male need. His tongue touched hers, dueled, then conquered. He tightened his grip, wanting her inside, where he could hold her forever.

His hand reached between them to clasp a breast, feeling its softness. A low moan escaped his throat at the searing pleasure radiating from his hand to the rest of his body. Slowly they sank beneath the water, the gently swelling waves closing over their heads as they drifted weightlessly. She wriggled a little in his arms. He leaned back and let her body rest on top of his as they gently moved up and down, imitating the actions of lovemaking. He felt like a firebrand that the icy water could not extinguish.

His own needs were so pressing that he could hardly control his actions. He gritted his teeth, trying to regain some control. But Alicia's sweet body called to him like an irresistible siren promising him pleasure and release.

Alicia closed her eyes; a sigh was caught between the space of two waves, echoing their sound. That sigh became his undoing.

"Alicia. My God."

She sprinkled kisses upon his face and shoulders. "I know. I know," she whispered. "Please...."

He needed no urging. Bathing suits were pushed aside. When he plunged into her warmth, long legs tightened around his body and clasped him. Breath even warmer than the Mexican breeze heated his skin. Their joining was bright, brilliant and as necessary to him as his beating heart. Her gasp of surprise heightened the response of the body that was tightening around his. He thought he'd burst and turned into brilliant colors to sprinkle the heavens. His mouth devoured hers, seeking to prolong the ecstasy that enveloped them.

When it was over, Jace held her tight, trying to catch his breath and clear his mind. His response had overwhelmed him and he wasn't certain what to do next. In fact he felt confused about a whole lot of things.

Suddenly Alicia was out of his arms. She showed him the creamy softness of her back as she slipped up her bathing-suit straps. Hastily he adjusted his own clothing, then touched her shoulder to draw her back into his arms.

Instead she backed off, disappearing into the froth of a wave. But Jace wasn't about to let her go. As she stroked, so did he. When he popped up beside her, they were both gasping for breath, and it wasn't all due to having been underwater. His heartbeat was thumping so loudly, he was amazed the water wasn't moving in synchrony.

She laughed nervously, letting her gaze dart everywhere but at him. "You're a very good seducer."

He thought of a million trite lines. Nothing less than honesty would work. "I didn't do it intentionally. You bring out needs in me that I didn't realize were there."

Her eyes widened, then crinkled delightfully at the corners. "You're not just good, with that touch of honest humility, you're great," she said, laughter tingeing her voice.

After such success, he couldn't help teasing her back. "Hell, maybe I should try more often."

"Maybe," she said, turning away to swim leisurely toward shore.

"Dinner?" he asked, joining her in a sidestroke so that he could see her.

"Are you sure about this?" she asked, suddenly serious. "I'm not making love with you again. And I'm not doing your building."

He'd forgotten about the damn building. What did she mean by saying she wasn't making love with him again? Had she found once enough? It wasn't nearly enough for him. But he had to take one step at a time. First he had to make her understand that she was going to see him again. "I'm sure. For today we're going to forget about business and sex." At her delighted smile, he amended his statement. "Well, at least the business."

"It's a deal. Dinner then."

"Anywhere in particular?"

"There's a restaurant that sits on the cliffs between here and a small fishing village down the road that has the most marvelous broiled shrimp and soup."

"What's your room number?"

Alicia hesitated, and Jace took her hand and helped her adjust her balance as they stood on the sandy bottom. "All I have to do is follow you upstairs. Isn't it a little silly to keep it a secret?"

"Room 814," she told him.

They walked toward the hotel, still holding hands. "I'll pick you up at seven," Jace announced, wrapping her towel around her shoulders. Small goose bumps rose on her arms, and he rubbed lightly.

"Fine." She took a step away from him. "I'll meet you in the lobby."

She still didn't trust him. And she was right not to, he thought wryly. "In the lobby," he repeated.

As she walked off, he picked up his own towel and rubbed briskly at his chest, trying to wipe away the memory of her breasts pressing there.

"Oh, and Jace?" she called over her shoulder.

He looked up, wishing he hadn't. She was beautiful. Her suit was backless, exposing a creamy skin he'd love to kiss all over. "Yes?" he asked hoarsely.

"You'd look great in a G-string." A smile peeped out and he chuckled.

"Thanks. So would you."

A blush covered her cheeks and she turned to walk quickly away. But there was a jauntiness to her stride.

He grinned. The woman was marvelous. Not only was she one great lover, but she kept her sense of command of the situation. An adult in every way. Everyone needed a compliment once in a while, and he'd treasure hers. It had come from a straightforward woman who said what was on her mind instead of mincing matters. He hadn't known how much he liked that until now, but did know how rare it was. Alicia was one of the few women he felt he might trust. *Might.* Doing it would be another matter.

But it was a start. Jace just wasn't sure where thoughts like that could lead. He hoped they might take him into her bed.

ALICIA WAS READY for dinner before seven, but was determined not to look eager by being early. Instead she paced her room. She'd decided on a champagne-pink sundress and strappy sandals. And because the breeze picked up when the sun went down, she chose an off-white, spidery-silk shawl. Every two minutes she checked in the mirror to insure her makeup and hair were okay. Her hair was down and slightly curled. With the evening winds, there was no sense in trying to keep a decent French knot. It would only be blown to wisps.

Every time she looked into the mirror, her mind reeled. She stared at her lips. Jace had made love to her. He'd kissed her and touched her and held her next to him in the clear, slick water. His clasp had been better than that of any imaginary lover, his touch erotic and demanding. Being with Jace surpassed anything she'd ever experienced.

That was what made it frightening.

All those years of sublimating desires for a home, a man who loved her, a family to love and be loved by. All those dreams she'd had to kill and bury in order to continue her professional life. Now they were like persistent ghosts, rising to haunt her in the face of Jace's passion.

It wasn't fair. Jace was a very unsuitable man, and she had no chance of making those dreams come true with the likes of him.

So why not enjoy what memories you can make— memories you can savor after he's gone?

It was as good an idea as any. Especially now that she'd already made love with him and knew what she'd be missing if she said no. She might as well enjoy the time she had with him, because it was ending soon enough. He'd leave when she did at the end of the week, if not sooner. She tried to pretend that the idea of not seeing Jace didn't hurt.

He was leaning against one of the pillars, watching the ocean through the wide-open windows when Alicia entered the lobby. He looked like an ad for a fine liquor or hand-tailored clothing. The man was devastatingly handsome.

When he saw her, he pushed away from the pillar and slipped his hands out of his pockets. A smile of appreciation curled his lips, and she had a hard time recalling the frown he'd worn when he bought her a drink in the bar at the hotel opening. She had made too many new memories of Jace Bartholomew to bother with the old ones.

His hand closed over her elbow as he led her toward the hotel front, where cabs were lined up. "You look beautiful," he said, his mouth close to her ear.

She glanced at him. "Thank you. Is that a criterion for your dates?"

"No, why?" He looked surprised.

"Because you've said that to me at least once every time we've met."

He let her step into the taxi first, then sat down beside her. After giving the name of the restaurant, he sat back and examined her until Alicia wanted to squirm. "Are you embarrassed by compliments?"

"Only when those giving them can't see that there's more to me than looks alone. Someday I'll be old, gray and wrinkled. Does that mean I'll be nothing then?"

"Never," he stated promptly. "It means that you'll be as beautiful for your age then as you are now."

For your age. The words brought back the difference between them. "No matter how old I'll be, you'll always be younger."

Jace stared out the window at the passing scenery. "That's right."

They spent the rest of the ride in silence.

But dinner was relaxing. By the time the waiter had seated them and they had ordered, the earlier tension was gone. Once more they had no problem in finding topics to discuss, business people they both knew. As long as Alicia steered clear of his family, Jace could talk about anything and make it interesting.

When he walked her back to her room, she felt tired, relaxed and happy. Her hand was clasped in one of his, her head rested lightly on his shoulder.

When they reached her door, she handed him the key and he opened it and drew her inside. It wasn't until they stood by her bed that she turned to face him. His hands came up to cradle her face between his palms.

With infinite tenderness, his lips brushed against her forehead. "You're worn out."

"Yes," she said with a sigh, closing her eyes. She tilted her head toward him while her arms crept around his waist. She swayed back and forth.

"You're exhausted." His voice grew even huskier, lightly scraping her nerves into a state of awareness.

"Yes."

"You've also had a little more wine than you're used to." He was almost whispering now.

"Yes," she whispered back.

"And I want you like I've never wanted another woman."

Eyes still closed, she smiled. "How nice."

"Are you going to do anything about it?"

"No," she said, slowly turning her head from side to side. "Are you?" It was a daring thing to say, but then she was in the arms of a man she was terribly attracted to. He'd already seduced her once in water and a second time with his conversation. Couldn't he see she wanted to be seduced by him? Couldn't he just take over and *do* it?

"Is that an invitation?"

She opened one eye. "I'm not sure."

He kissed her again on the forehead. "You're not sure of anything, lady mine." There was a chuckle in his voice.

With expert hands he took off her shawl and undid her zipper. Then he turned her until her knees hit the bed. "Sit down," he said.

Before she realized what was going on, she was perched on the end of the bed and Jace was undoing her strappy sandals. A cool breeze touched her back and she shivered.

"Cold?"

She nodded, watching him through half-closed eyes. He bent his head and lights glimmered in his dark hair. Too tired to resist, she reached out and felt its springy vitality.

Jace looked up, her shoes in his hands. "Do you know what you're doing?"

"I always wanted to touch your hair and see what it felt like."

"And?" he prompted softly.

"It feels good. Thick and springy and vibrant. As if it's got a life of its own."

"Damn." His gaze caught hers, his eyes telling her in intimate detail what he'd like to do to her. Her breath caught in her throat at the thought. She felt more than saw his reaction.

"I give up, Alicia. I'm only human," he said, rising. He bent and touched his lips to hers. But it wasn't with the gentleness of earlier—it was the urgency of *now*—the kind of kiss that demanded and staked a claim. It was perfect.

Alicia curled her arms around his neck.

He tumbled, flattening her against the firm mattress. Giggles spilled from Alicia's mouth, adding to the laughter that made Jace's chest rumble against her breast.

A few minutes later he touched his forehead to hers. "I don't believe this. I've never laughed with a half-naked, slightly tipsy and very tired woman in my arms. What is it that makes you so different?"

"Is making love always supposed to be so serious?" she asked, brushing a lock of his hair from his forehead, only to watch in fascination as the errant curl slipped back.

"Yes."

She grinned. "For me, too. At least, usually it is," she amended. "Not that we're really making love . . ."

"Yes, we are," he told her emphatically. "It's too late now, Alicia. You're already committed."

She wasn't about to argue, just ask questions. "Here? Now?"

He grinned. "Yes."

She shrugged nonchalantly, but felt a blush climb its way up her neck and cheeks. "Okay."

His laughter filled the air once more. She didn't know why but had to join in. It felt so wonderful to be with him!

"We're getting ready to make mad, passionate love and all you can say is okay?" he asked.

"It's an agreement, isn't it?"

"You're right," he affirmed. "I'll take it before you change your mind."

His lips touched hers, then pulled away. "Ready or not, here I come," he murmured, then took possession of her lips.

From that point on, Alicia forgot about laughing, but relearned the art of sensuous touching. She was surrounded by the dark, wonderful scent and sound of Jace Bartholomew, and for the life of her couldn't recall what it was like to be in a big bed alone. But some small part knew she would remember soon enough, so she might as well enjoy him now.

6

THE REST OF THE WEEK was a hazy, wonderful dream. Alicia spent every moment—waking and sleeping—with Jace. But she insisted that he had to keep his room. In case his brothers or his office called, the messages would be received there. He agreed reluctantly, disappearing only to change clothes and make an occasional phone call.

On the third day of their vacation, a bellboy delivered a large envelope from Trace, the private detective she'd hired. Much as she wanted to tear into it, she couldn't. At least not while Jace was around. She was feeling stupid for having him investigated, but the unknown contents of the envelope were also terribly tantalizing. When she had discovered that Jace intended to share her vacation she had decided it was time to use her brain instead of her heart—and learn whether the rumours about Jace were truth or fiction.

It wasn't until the fourth day that Jace left her for long enough. Quickly she tore it open and read through the contents, then lay on the bed on her stomach and flipped through the well-stuffed file. Much of it she already knew. He'd been raised by a domineering mother who was in and out of fashionable sanitariums for an undisclosed mental illness.

The family dynamics were interesting. In childhood, Jace had won several awards for team sports: doubles tennis, baseball and relay track teams. Although Brad had traveled extensively with his father during his teen years, Jace hadn't, instead staying at home and acting as big brother to Cam. Brad had been raised like an only child, so it was no wonder Jace had slipped into the role of family caretaker.

Everything he'd done as a youth cried out for a family. Alicia, an only child herself, saw all the same symptoms she had displayed. Had he been lonely? Had he cried himself to sleep at night, wondering why his parents didn't give him the love he craved?

He'd married a girl he'd met in college. With six other brothers and sisters, his wife had come from a large, rowdy family. They had one child, Meagan Marie, now nine years old. Four years after their wedding they divorced and his wife had really taken him to the cleaners. From the accusations in the divorce transcript, she obviously hated him with every fiber in her being and sought to keep him from his child. His response had been to remain stoically silent throughout the whole ordeal. His ex-wife had even accused him of having several affairs, but nothing had been proven.

Since Jace's divorce he'd had no lasting relationships. No woman had lasted longer than three or four months. That piece of information somehow hurt Alicia more than any other she'd run across.

Was she destined to be yet another of these nameless women? Would he tire of her, too, and leave her crying? She didn't think she could stand that. If she felt involved now, how much more would her emotional stability be at risk in three or four months? In that length of time she might become so involved, so wrapped up in him that he would probably be able to tear her to shreds with a single, careless look.

Recalling that she had walked into this relationship with her eyes open, she saw now that she'd be to blame if she got hurt. She knew what his reputation was and despite this knowledge had gotten involved.

Alicia stared out at the ocean. A soft, warm breeze caressed her skin. She remembered their underwater lovemaking and her heart missed a beat. Okay. So she'd gotten more involved than she had planned to. She just wouldn't allow herself to care too much, she finally decided, recognizing a fool's statement but not knowing what else to do. *Not* spending the rest of her vacation with him was a horrible thought. He was here. She was here. For only three more days. They would spend them together. *And then their affair would be over.*

Slipping the file into its large manila envelope, Alicia placed it at the bottom of her suitcase for safekeeping. For now this was her fantasy—she might as well enjoy it! She heard Jace's special knock and knew a smile lighted her eyes as she opened the door. He swept her into his arms. Only her heart felt the tenderness of a bruise no one could see....

THEY FROLICKED in the sun-dappled sea, ran along the white sands, lay under the coconut palms. At night, Jace possessively clasped her hand in his and they strolled on the moonlit beach. When they slipped into bed, they made love. After the loving they curled up spoon fashion and slept like children. His hand always touched her. Her breath always caressed his skin, her fingertips skimmed his shoulders and hips. She couldn't touch him enough. He couldn't have enough of their lovemaking. It was the perfect combination.

Always was the word that persistently hovered on the outer edges of Alicia's mind. She ignored it, much as one ignored a misbehaving child, refusing to think of the past, the future or the consequences.

Silent on their last night in Ixtapa, they walked along the beach to the point where the silver sea met the grayness of sand. The dull roar of the surf seemed to mock Alicia. It would end, it would end, it would end....

She'd known this day was coming, had just fooled herself into believing that it wouldn't be so hard to say goodbye, go back home and get on with the reality of her everyday life.

Jace's footsteps slowed. His hand tightened around hers and she turned to him inquiringly. With slow and easy movements he wrapped his arms around her waist, bringing her so close that she felt his heartbeat against her breast.

"Come back with me." His voice was low, rasping.

Her hand stroked his cheek. She couldn't think of any answer other than the one she'd been giving herself all week. "Impossible."

"No, it's not. If you took the job on my building, you'd be in Chicago for at least three months."

Her fingers trailed down his jaw to the open collar of his shirt. "And then what, Jace?"

"I don't know."

"Wouldn't it be better to end this now?" she asked softly, hearing her own frustration as she spoke. "This relationship can't continue. We know that."

His hand covered hers, pressing her palm to his flesh. "Probably," he muttered hoarsely. His blue eyes stared down at her. How could she have thought his expression unreadable? Right now her skin was burning with the searing intimacy of his look. "But I don't want to end it. Do you?"

She shook her head. "No," she admitted. "I don't want to, either."

"Then come back with me."

"I can't."

"Why can't you? You don't really have a pressing contract to fulfill. I have a building that needs doing, and you do buildings."

"This relationship isn't going to get any better," Alicia protested. "Neither of us have any plans for love or marriage. Why go any further?" She waited for him to correct her. She prayed for it.

He grinned. "Because it's not over. I still want to wake up tomorrow and find you curled up next to me. I still want to turn over and nudge you into awakeness. I still want to walk with you along the shoreline." His hands grasped her slim shoulders, and he tightened his grip. "Let's try it. I get my building done, you get a good commission. And we *both* get to continue this relationship for a while. The top floor of the building even hosts a VIP suite, although it needs renovation, too. You can stay there and be close to the action. It might even help you complete the work faster."

"And then what?" She knew hopelessness tinged her voice, but couldn't help it. This hurt—a lot. But if it hurt now, what would it feel like in three months? *Find out*, a small voice said. *What have you got to lose except loneliness?*

Jace shrugged. He rested his chin against the top of her head. "I don't know," he admitted at last. "But we won't know if we end it here."

"I'll think about it," Alicia conceded. She had to end things, but like Jace she wasn't ready. Not yet.

"Say yes," he demanded. "Say yes and come with me."

"I'll think about it," she hedged, still unsure—and unwilling to let Jace railroad her into an answer she might regret.

Jace sighed heavily, but loosened his grip. "I'll give you time, Alicia. You've got until tomorrow morning at nine-thirty. That's when the company jet is flying me back to Chicago."

She wished she didn't know. Until now their departure had only been a hazy idea that would become reality sometime in the future. Now it had a time and a date. Their story had an ending. Paradise didn't—couldn't—last forever.

"Damn!"

It was uttered under her breath, but Jace heard it and laughed. "At least you admit to some of the frustration I've been feeling."

"Just a little," she admitted, turning to walk toward the ocean. She crossed her arms over her chest, warding off the chill she always felt when she wasn't in Jace's embrace. She was becoming addicted.

Jace came up behind her and enfolded her in his arms. In a comfortable silence they watched the undulating motion of the water. "This is crazy."

"Yes."

"Let's go to our room."

"Yes."

Holding hands, they walked back through the hotel.

Alicia woke up in the middle of the night. Bright moonlight ribboned their room. Jace was curled around her, one hand at her waist, his warm breath on her neck. Staring into the semidarkness, she wondered how she had become used to sleeping with him so quickly. Only six days had passed since they had become lovers . . . but it felt so right.

Jace stirred, stroking his hand the length of her hip and sending out wonderful messages. "Alicia?"

She sighed. "Yes?"

His hand moved to cup a breast. "Are you all right?"

She realized she'd made her decision. "I'm fine. And I'm going to decorate your building." What other choice did she have? She didn't want to leave Jace yet. Not yet.

One hand pressed lightly upon her shoulder until she turned and stared into his eyes. "You won't be sorry." It was a promise he wouldn't be able to keep, she knew.

Alicia chuckled bitterly. "Yes, I will."

Gently he bit her bottom lip, tugging it into his mouth. "You won't be hurt. I promise."

Vows spoken in the dark weren't meant to be kept in the light of day. She'd learned that at an early age. But these circumstances had gotten out of control, just like her emotions. She had no desire to run away and no will to resist. Staying with Jace might be all wrong for her, but it was what she wanted.

ALICIA HAD CAUSE to wonder at her decision as the Bartholomew Corporation's extravagantly decorated plane flew toward Chicago. Perhaps she'd been half-crazy and just a little dull-witted to commit herself to such a scheme.

There weren't any direct flights to Chicago from Ixtapa, and Jace had decided he needed to return immediately. Cashing in her ticket, he'd arranged for the family jet to take them home. No use wasting time by spending most of the day traveling.

Alicia could only nod her head in agreement. What did he know? Most of the world didn't travel this way, but the Bartholomews were—different.

Jace sipped his coffee as he watched her. "Second thoughts?" he asked, his tone distant. He could have been talking to the hired help, Alicia reflected.

"Not at all," she denied, wondering why she was lying. "But it was folly for me to go directly to Chicago. I should have gone home first and packed the things I need. Then I could have joined you in a week or so."

"Or come up with a good excuse not to join me at all." He stared into his cup, then looked at her again. She was surprised to see vulnerability in his eyes. She wasn't sure how to handle it. "Is it so hard to be with me?"

This was a side of Jace he'd never revealed before. "You know better."

His brows rose. The expression he'd worn the first night they'd spoken came to mind. He was withdrawing right in front of her, changing from a vulnerable, little boy to a distant, aloof man. "Really? How am I supposed to know that? By the way you flirt with me? By how often you tell me how much you love me? By your reluctance to leave my side?"

"That's not fair!" Alicia protested, angry that he wanted emotions from her, emotions he wasn't prepared to offer. "You wouldn't ask yourself those questions, so why expect me to answer them?" She stood and walked the length of the living area. "If you want openness in this relationship, you'd better be the first one to be open. Don't ask me to do what you wouldn't."

His expression remained bland, but she saw a small light of admiration in his eyes. "Fair enough. Let's do the best we can with the circumstances, Alicia. Meanwhile..." He gestured to the side wall where a telephone stood on a desk. "Why don't you call your office and make the necessary arrangements? With a little luck, you could have everything in a day."

"And the Bartholomew Corporation will have that amount added to their bill."

"Of course." A small smile played around his mouth. But instead of saying anything else, he picked up a copy of a business paper and began reading. Alicia made her phone call.

They arrived in Chicago a little after noon. The corporate limousine picked them up, whisked them across town and dropped them in front of the Bartholomew Building.

Scaffolding hung from the top. Men in what looked like space suits were painstakingly sandblasting one square of limestone at a time. When she looked at Jace, he commented, "The exterior work has been going on since last month. You have an appointment with the architect tomorrow."

"How was that arranged?" she asked, ready for an argument. She'd said she was coming to Chicago only this morning, so how had he known to make that appointment—unless he had been arrogantly sure her answer would be yes?

"I called this morning while you were in the shower." His statement was bland, his tone preoccupied as he led her into the building and toward the bank of elevators. "He was thrilled to death with your acceptance. He wants to go over with you some of the decisions he's already made."

That took the wind out of her sails. She'd forgotten he'd been on the phone half the morning.

The interior of the building caught her attention. True to the photos, the lobby was a disaster. Oil-starved picture paneling crawled up the walls like a dark blight. Twenty-four feet of it, at least. The ceiling's ornate molding was in an entirely different style, as was the gray marble floor.

"Good grief!" Alicia muttered.

She saw Jace follow her gaze, a rueful gleam in his eyes. "Amazing, isn't it?" He ushered her into the elevator and pushed the top-floor button. "We've owned this building for fifteen years, but we only moved our offices here about a year ago. I thought I could live with it for a while, but I was mistaken."

"It's a challenge," Alicia said quietly. Her heart was pumping with excitement. What she could do with this building! She loved a challenge and this would be a big one. And that made it fun.

When the doors opened, Alicia stepped into a drab reception area. Jace's hand on the small of her back guided her toward another elevator against the side wall. "Awful, isn't it?" he muttered.

She didn't have a chance to answer. A short, stocky, older woman aimed herself at them. "Mr. Bartholomew!" Her voice cracked as she called his name.

Without turning, Jace stopped and sighed. "Yes, Virginia?"

"Will you be returning to your office soon?" she asked, peering over her bifocals as she stepped to his side. She did not look at Alicia.

Jace grinned. "Did you miss me?"

"Yes." It was a matter-of-fact statement.

"Aren't you interested in learning who this beautiful woman is?" Jace asked.

Alicia hid her grin. Jace was clearly baiting Virginia. This was obviously an ongoing battle.

"Only if you want me to be," came the other woman's answer.

"Alicia, meet my secretary and right hand, Virginia. Virginia, this is the commercial decorator, Alicia Dumont."

"How do you do," Alicia said, extending her hand.

"Thank goodness," Virginia replied, clasping her hand in a warm grasp, changing her entire demeanor. "You're needed here. I'm glad you decided to take our project before three-quarters of our staff leaves."

"It's not that bad!" Jace protested, defending what he had maligned just moments ago.

"Yes, it is," Virginia retorted, not looking at him but studying Alicia. "Whatever you need, ask me. I also have a woman from our typing pool who'll make an excellent assistant. If you need help, I'll send her up."

"Up?" Alicia was puzzled.

Virginia gave a perfunctory nod as she reached for the elevator button. "Yes. To the VIP suite. I have the cleaning crew up there now. Aside from an ancient kitchen and bath, it has a spacious bedroom, living room and another space laughably called the office because it holds a desk and an empty, antiquated file cabinet."

"Thank you, Virginia," Jace said in a dismissive tone.

"You're welcome." When she looked at her employer, a smile softened her face. "And I'll be expecting a visit from you soon," she said, returning her attention to Alicia. "Meanwhile, just dial my extension if you need anything."

"Thank you," Alicia called as Jace firmly took her arm and led her into the elevator.

"This is the only way you can get to the top floor," he explained. "The other elevator only hits the offices."

Alicia wasn't interested in the elevator. "Is that your only secretary?"

He sighed. "Yes." There was a defensive tone to his voice.

"I like her," she said.

Jace looked surprised. "Why?"

"Because she's obviously a woman who gets the job done. Because she thinks of ways to get it done quicker and more efficiently." Alicia hesitated a moment. "And she's obviously very possessive and protective of you."

His grin was sheepish. "You might say that. Others call her the battle-ax and get frustrated trying to get through her to me. But she knows what to do and does it well."

Alicia chuckled as she stepped off the elevator. "Apparently you're worth more to her than a paycheck. And your credibility is sagging. You can't hate all women if you feel that way about her."

They walked into a large room decorated in Danish furniture from the fifties.

Jace put down her suitcase beside the couch. "What makes you think I hate women?"

"The entire world knows your secret, Jace. You blame women for your family problems. You discard them when you're tired of them."

"You make me sound like a house cleaner changing air fresheners. That's not true."

Alicia peeked around the corner at the kitchen. Virginia was right. The refrigerator looked as if it was one of the first electrical appliances. "Yes, it is."

"Then why do you have anything to do with me?"

She stuck her head into the bathroom. A claw-footed tub? She loved it and vowed to have her first bubble bath in years. Alone. She needed to have some distance from Jace if she was going to be able to concentrate on the job. "Because I always wondered what it would be like to be with a younger man. Now I know."

He grabbed her hand as she started toward the bedroom. "Hold it!" She turned in his arms and faced him, resting her hands lightly on his chest. He was still wearing casual clothes, something she guessed he didn't do often enough. The blue knit shirt clung to his muscled body, outlining the form she was beginning to love too much.

"Now tell me the real reason you went to bed with a man who's supposed to hate women." His tone was teasing, but the look in his eyes wasn't.

For the first time she felt shy. That was ridiculous, she told herself. She should be able to take charge of the situation, be in control. "It's very simple," she finally managed to say. "You are a handsome, intelligent, charming man when you want to be and very sexy. Now why would any woman, young or old, turn that down?"

His face looked like a slowly building thundercloud. "Age has nothing to do with our going to bed together. We're both past the age of consent and that's all that matters." His grip tightened. "And if you have any other cute little cop-out phrases, keep them to yourself. I want the truth."

"For someone who gives the appearance of not wanting to discuss emotions, you sure are demanding where others are concerned!" she exclaimed, lacing her voice with sarcasm in defense. Although he looked angry, Alicia sensed his need to hear words that soothed his ego right now. It was comforting to think that he was as vulnerable as she was—at least as far as this relationship went.

"Am I supposed to be a challenge to your ego? Is that it?" he demanded.

"No, although I'd be lying if I didn't admit it's flattering to know a younger man wants to make love to me, when there are so many younger women out there."

Some of the tension eased from his muscles. "Thank you for that, at least." His eyes focused on her lips. "But youth—or lack of it—has nothing to do with what's between us. You're beautiful, intelligent, and one of the most honest women I've met. That alone makes you a rarity. I still can't believe I found you."

"God gifted you with a silver tongue."

He grinned. Alicia felt tension turning into need.

Her hands slid from his chest up to his neck, then cupped the sides of his jaw. His look was one of passion, pleasure and a touch of wonder. She basked in it like a new flower reaching for sunshine. It felt wonderful to be thought of that way, even if it was also a little frightening. What if she couldn't live up to his expectations?

"You're a rare jewel, Alicia. I'm not sure I believe I'm really with you."

"And you're a very unsuitable man, Jace. I'm not sure I should be with you at all," she said, smiling in spite of herself.

"For someone who's always saying no, you feel wonderful in my arms. And even better in my bed."

She knew her cheeks dimpled as she responded. His eyes sought her mouth again, and she wished he would kiss her. "You're not bad yourself."

"That's probably a gross understatement." He bent and brushed her lips with a stroke as light as a summer cobweb. When he pulled away, she followed his movement. He did it again. "And you taste good, too."

"Mmm," she murmured, feeling as if her bones were turning to a thick, syrupy liquid. She arched her neck, asking for the kiss she now craved. A low chuckle told her he knew what she wanted.

But Alicia was too impatient to wait. Standing on tiptoe, she reached up and pulled his head down. Then Jace took the lead. His mouth captured hers and deepened the kiss until his desire was as plain as her own. His arms tightened, pulling her in to his body, filling her curves with hardness, her hollows with heat. Alicia closed her eyes. Delicious colors of sensation lighted her insides and she leaned into Jace even more.

A moan escaped his throat, echoing into their mouths as they fused. Crackling sounds filled the living room, but nothing really registered until Jace reluctantly pulled away.

He lifted his head. "Yes, Virginia," he called patiently. Alicia opened her eyes and looked around until she found the square speaker of a wall intercom not two feet from them.

"You have a meeting in the boardroom in half an hour. Your suit and shirt are in the penthouse closet." Her tone was crisp. The sound from the box was scratchy and loud, with a grating whistle in the background.

"Thank you, Virginia. I'll be down in time," Jace replied patiently.

"Right."

The static stopped, the connection cut.

Jace sighed, forcing himself to pull away from the warmth of Alicia's soft body. Every nerve in him screamed out for the culmination of what they had begun. He wanted this woman like he'd never wanted another, and wasn't used to denying himself—even for business. But, he didn't remember ever having these desires while doing business, either.

Her hand feathered across his brow. "Are you all right?" Her voice was soft with concern and he loved the thought that she cared.

He smiled. "I'm fine. Will you be okay up here? I know it's ancient, but it's clean and close to work. And to me."

"It will do fine. However, I think it will probably be one of the first places I start. This area isn't really ready to work in."

"Call Virginia if you have any problems. I'll be up later. I think the meeting's going to last until nine or ten, at least."

She nodded her understanding. Business had always taken precedence over her personal life, too. "Get dressed or you'll be late."

When he'd gone, Alicia walked around the apartment, touching the old rolltop desk, brushing her fingers across the long, 1950's bureau and pulling back curtains to allow sunshine to paint everything in brighter colors.

The only good thing about the apartment was the view. Chicago lay below on one side, its high-rise buildings dominating the landscape. To the other side was a view of Lake Michigan that seemed to go on forever. Two skimpy trees in large concrete planters stood like tired sentinels on either side of the terrace. She couldn't help but think they'd do better with water and food.

Uttering a wistful sigh, Alicia picked up the phone and dialed the extension number Jace had left. When Virginia answered, Alicia asked for the supplies she needed. She also asked for the secretary Virginia had spoken of earlier.

After the phone call she stared out the window and brooded. She was getting too involved with Jace and wasn't sure what to do about it. She should have said no to coming with him to Chicago, but there was, after all, nothing else she could have done. She was along for the ride now.

She reached for a pencil and paper. Regardless of regrets, it was time to get to work.

7

JACE WATCHED ALICIA with the architect, Howard Ambrose, marveling at her grasp of the blueprints. Until now he'd never thought about how much she had to know to do her job well. He hadn't even considered what it meant to be one of the top commercial decorators in the field. And if he'd still had any reservations about making her his choice, the architect had put those to rest. Howard treated Alicia with respect, showing Jace that she was more than equal to the task.

Her vision of what the building could be had Howard exclaiming his enthusiasm. At that Jace felt an irrational amount of anger toward the older, more sophisticated architect, who, he thought, was looking at Alicia with more than a professional eye.

Couldn't she see the man was a pain in the butt? And that he wore a wedding ring? To be sure, Jace knew the wedding ring was a fake, meant to keep away women who were looking for commitment rather than a slight affair. Howard was known for his love 'em-and-leave 'em attitude, never allowing himself to be seen twice with the same woman. But Alicia couldn't know that.

Just then Howard slipped his hand over Alicia's and gave it a light squeeze. Alicia continued talking, pointing out more problems with the lobby, but pulled her hand away to reach for another drawing.

Jace breathed a sigh of relief.

He contributed little to the meeting other than an occasional agreement. He'd already approved the architect's renderings, and knew nothing about decorating. Normally he would have let them have this meeting in private, but refused to leave Alicia alone with this guy.

Howard tried to hold Alicia's hand again. Alicia smiled sweetly and withdrew it from his grasp to point at something. Didn't she realize what a pass was?

Jace felt his temper build and took a deep breath to contain it. It wouldn't do either of them any good if he lost his cool. Two minutes later, when Howard appeared to stroke Alicia's cheek in saying goodbye, Jace decided he didn't need any rapport with his architect.

"Keep your hands to yourself," he growled.

Architect and decorator looked at him in surprise. Well, almost surprise. He had to admit that Alicia looked more angry.

"Sorry, Jace. But it's not your place to tell me what to do." Howard's tone was militant. "That's up to Alicia."

"Unless I say otherwise," Jace retorted, not even looking at Alicia. He sensed her anger now and hoped she had finally realized what kind of man the damn architect was.

"Excuse me," Alicia said pointedly to Jace, then turned her back to him and faced the older man, one hand on his jacket sleeve. "Thank you for asking, but I'm sorry, Howard. I already have plans."

Jace stared hard at her. Howard had asked her out and he hadn't heard it!

"Maybe we'd better have a discussion, Howard," he suggested, making his tone as threatening as possible.

Alicia pivoted, narrowing her eyes as she glared at Jace. "Perhaps *you* and *I* had better have a talk instead, Mr. Bartholomew." Her tone was light, but the look was dark.

Jace finally realized he'd goofed, but wasn't sure how. All he knew was that he wanted Howard to leave and Alicia to wrap her arms around him. He didn't really want to punch Howard on the nose. Not hard, at least.

"I'll see you in the morning," the architect murmured, laying the plans upon the table. "Meanwhile, go ahead and study these. You know what I'm after."

Alicia continued to stare at Jace. "Thank you, I will."

Howard walked out the door and shut it behind him. His smug look barely registered with Jace.

The moment the click sounded, telling Alicia that she and Jace were alone, she turned on him, eyes blazing in anger.

"Don't you ever interfere with my relationships with business associates again!"

He was incredulous. "Don't you realize he was propositioning you? It wasn't just a matter of working on this building with him. He wanted to play house with your sweet little body. He couldn't tell you the color of your eyes, but knew exactly what shape your breasts were. For God's sake, Alicia! That man wasn't just playing at being a wolf in sheep's clothing!"

Her eyes widened. "Even an idiot would know that! Great balls of fire, what do you take me for?" She placed her hands on her hips and stalked toward him. For a moment he thought of an angry cat, but Alicia was surely too sweet for that. She must be bluffing.

He smiled in what he hoped was his most charming manner. "You don't know men like I do, especially that one. I've known him for years and he's the best in his business. But when it comes to women, he goes through them like women use Kleenex at a tearjerker movie."

"That's his business, not yours," Alicia retorted, her expression resembling a stone wall. "And I happen to think one hell of a lot more about women who cry in movies than I do of meddling, macho men."

"When that gray-haired lech starts handling my decorator, he makes it my business."

"Wrong!" Alicia exclaimed. "That's your decorator's business! Whatever happens is only between Howard and me. *You* have nothing to do with it."

Frustration boiled up inside him. Couldn't she see that most men were after the same thing—a beautiful woman in their bed? She couldn't be that blind! "You don't understand."

"Unless you also think I'm too dumb to see the implications here, I understand perfectly. You want to play the protective macho man. But I work with men every day. I have to deal with them as if there's no man around to protect me. Because there isn't."

He folded his arms across his chest to stop himself taking hold of her. "Then there should be."

"Why?" she queried sarcastically. "So the big, strong man can baby-sit me for the rest of my life? That's what it would take." She smiled, but there was no mirth in her eyes. "So you see, Jace, unless you're willing to escort me everywhere except the ladies' bathroom, you'd better back off and let me handle my own affairs."

"It's not right," he muttered in frustration. What was so wrong with wanting to protect Alicia?

One long red fingernail lightly poked at his chest. "You are either very chauvinist or very dumb. I can't decide which. But if you want to believe that women are the weaker sex, then believe it around someone else. Not this lady—and not on my working time."

Words failed him. He wasn't sure how to explain his problem with this setup. Hell, he couldn't even figure out how to describe it to himself. And no matter what else he said, he was sure she'd have a comeback. His business instinct warned him to leave the topic alone. His emotions, however, were out of whack. They kept telling him to stand firm until she saw things his way, even though he knew it was unlikely.

"Alicia," he began, furrowing his brow at the sudden image of Alicia on a date with Howard. "I don't want you going anywhere with him."

He could tell from her wide eyes that she was as stunned by his words as he was. Now he'd done it. Telling a woman what to do always made her angry, and this one was obviously no exception.

Instead of speaking, Alicia turned on her heel and marched out the door.

Her silence spoke more than a thousand words.

Jace let out the breath he'd been holding and slumped into his leather desk chair.

He'd goofed. He knew it, yet he hadn't been able to stop himself. "Bartholomew, what the hell's the matter with you?"

He'd pushed as if waiting for Alicia to walk out, so in fact he'd expected more of a reaction than he'd got. She could have thrown the job back at him or slapped his face. She could even have screamed and yelled at him.

Instead she'd just walked out of his office without letting him know her intentions.

That worried him.

ALICIA CLOSED Jace's door as quietly as possible, then stood still, taking deep breaths to slow her erratic heartbeat. The man deserved an award for being the best example of a male chauvinistic pig.

Jace's secretary stopped on her way past, a sheaf of papers in her hand. "Are you all right?"

"No." Alicia ran a hand around her neck, willing herself to calm down. "I'd love to strangle your boss for being a throwback to the Dark Ages, but I might ruin things for some other woman seeking revenge. I'm sure I can't be the only one who feels this way."

Virginia laughed outright at Alicia's words. "No one ever taught him how to fight in a relationship, so he takes on personal battles like a boardroom dispute," she agreed. "But if you're willing to train him, I'll help."

"Teach him how to fight?"

The older woman nodded. "You know. Stick to what he's feeling rather than what he can blame you or others for. Whatever you decide to do, I'll back you up one hundred percent."

Alicia tilted her head and stared at the other woman. She obviously cared for Jace. "Why do you want me to do this?"

"Because he's the best businessman I know, but he's in kindergarten when it comes to relationships. And if he's ever going to be happy, he has to learn how to fight with someone he cares about. I think you're the one to help teach him because I saw how he looked at you. And you know what I'm talking about when I say he has to learn. Some women don't understand that you can train a man to grow." Virginia shrugged. "Men are no different on that level than women are. We all want to please, we just have to be shown how to do so occasionally."

"He's a true gem in the rough," Alicia commented dryly.

Virginia nodded her agreement. "He is," she confirmed. "And one of the nicest people I know. He just needs a little female persuasion, that's all."

Alicia hated to admit how much the idea appealed to her. But she didn't have to. By the look on Jace's secretary's face, she could tell she'd been read. "Let me think about it." She smiled. "I'm sure I'll come up with something."

The older woman smiled. "Good. Now would you like to meet the assistant I picked out for you? Her name is Kendall and she's just right for the job."

"If I ever needed help, it's now," Alicia declared fervently.

"I'll introduce you to her now. Then you can both get started."

Introductions took place in a room where twenty other secretaries were sitting in front of computers. Cables littered the floor, then ran up the walls. It looked just like an ad for a computer company.

Kendall was more than Alicia could have hoped for. She was pretty, bright and eager to begin. She even had some limited experience with decorators. That meant she knew rules were to be followed and creativity needed to be channeled in the right direction. Alicia's smile answered Virginia's smug grin. Virginia had chosen well and deserved to bask in the glow of her wise decision.

Armed with pencils and pads of papers, Alicia led the way to her apartment, making notes of supplies she needed as she went. "And I have to get you a card for the elevator. You'll be working up here with me for the time being," she told Kendall, scribbling down that thought under the heading of items to talk to Jace's secretary about.

She wished she hadn't thought of Jace and cast a covert glance at Kendall. Not quite as tall as herself, Kendall was even thinner. Her long dark hair tumbled wildly about her slender shoulders, making her heart-shaped face resemble that of a waif. Although it was alive with excitement, she nonetheless looked wiped out, as if she barely had enough energy to set one foot in front of the other and walk down the long hall.

Opening the doors to her apartment, Alicia dumped the armload of materials onto the dining-room table and turned to face the girl.

"If this job is too much for you, Kendall, then I need to know now. I can't afford to get halfway through this project and have you back out or become ill."

Kendall's expression was determined. "I know I look anemic," she replied, "but I'm not. I'm just thin. I also happen to have two children at home—Mandy is seven and Dan is three—who take up an enormous amount of energy. They keep me slim."

Alicia ignored the pang of jealousy she felt whenever children were discussed. "I'm slim," she corrected with a smile. "You're skinny."

"All right. Skinny. But I'm strong and capable and can think quickly on my feet. You won't find a more eager assistant in Chicago."

Leaning a hip against the table, Alicia crossed her arms and studied the other woman. Kendall stared back, looking her squarely in the eye. If this was the way Kendall did business, she wouldn't be intimidated by workers or architects. That was enough to tip the scales in her favor.

"Okay," Alicia agreed. "You can do the job as long as you do it well."

Kendall's response was practical. "What do I do first, boss?"

"Tomorrow I want you to take me on a tour of the building and tell me everything you know or have heard in rumor."

"Can do. What else?"

"Can you read blueprints?"

Kendall nodded. "A little. My husband was a draftsman."

"What does he do now?"

Her expression grew somber so quickly that it took Alicia by surprise. "He died two years ago in an auto accident."

"I'm sorry," Alicia murmured. The girl was too young to have known that kind of tragedy.

Kendall shrugged. "He brought it on himself. He was drunk, leaving a fun time at a local bar. The woman in the car with him was paralyzed from the waist down."

"And you were left with two small children."

"And an insurance policy that paid off the house and car, but left no money for bills or anything else." Kendall's voice was bitter now. "Obviously he didn't think he was going to need insurance."

"And that's why you're working now?"

"Yes. When Jim was alive, he wouldn't hear of me working. Now that he's gone, I have no choice."

"Do you like your job here?"

"I love it," Kendall said quickly. She stared out the window. "I used to feel guilty for wanting to work while I had babies at home. I know my working is tough on the kids, but I don't feel guilty anymore, because now

I don't have a choice. Not if I want to put food in their tummies and shoes on their feet."

"Amazing," Alicia murmured. "As women we're always ready to berate ourselves for not giving enough, but I've never seen a man do that. When does a reporter ever ask a man who takes care of the children while he works? Or how he manages his career and his home life?"

Turning to the blueprints, she unfolded them on the table.

"We're beginning on this floor first. This is what the architect wants to do, and we need to know his steps intimately before we can determine our own. We'll have to be a jump ahead of him all the time. We also need to take a good long look at the lobby tomorrow. Some people may never get any farther than the lobby, so it will have to be the most eye-catching place in the building."

"I understand," Kendall said, studying the papers in front of her.

"And I need you to contact the architect's office in the morning and ask for any copies of the original specifications on the building."

"Will they have them?"

"They'll have them," Alicia stated confidently. "Any architect who's worth his salt digs up the originals. That tells him where the steel is, how the windows were designed and a thousand other details he'd have to spend time and money on discovering if he wants to do a good job.

"And then I need any newspaper articles written about the building when it opened. The library should have files on that, along with other information regarding the decor of the time."

"Okay, boss." Kendall scribbled furiously on one of the pads. "Anything else?"

"Copies of local magazines between 1900 and 1906. I want to see the interiors of Chicago homes and businesses."

"Gotcha." Kendall looked up. "What else?"

Alicia was pleased by her eagerness. "Go home and get some sleep. From now on you'll be running."

Kendall looked at her watch. "But it's only three o'clock."

"From now on," Alicia said softly, "you get paid for working for me, not for putting in x number of hours."

Kendall's bright blue eyes widened. "All right."

"And there will be plenty of nights that you'll be working late. So you might as well enjoy the time now. Will your baby-sitter be able to work late if you're here late?"

"No problem. She wants me to get ahead—probably so she can ask me for a raise," Kendall said with a laugh, dropping the pad and pen onto the table and gathering the roll of blueprints in her arms. "I'll see you tomorrow morning."

"Tomorrow morning," Alicia echoed before the young woman walked out the door. Tomorrow would come soon enough. Right now she needed a shower and time to get ready for dinner with Jace.

Despite their argument earlier, she knew he'd be there on time. He had honestly believed that guarding her from that wolf of an architect was the honest and honorable thing to do. Virginia was right, she just had to teach him how to fight.

Her heartbeat raced at the thought that Jace would be with her any minute. Her shower was quick, brisk and hot. Within five minutes Alicia was turning off the faucet and slipping a plush, cherry-red bath sheet around her body, fastening it securely under one arm.

When she stepped out of the tub, her eyes fell upon Jace. He was leaning against the open door, feet crossed, his jacket slung over one arm. A white silk shirt tucked into dark pants emphasized the muscles beneath. His expression was tender.

He opened his arms. "Come here," he ordered softly. "I need to touch you."

She was too old to play games, Alicia thought as she walked into his embrace. His arms wrapped around her like a silken vise. She rested her cheek against the hardness of him, her fingers feeling muscles tense under her touch. He sighed and she felt his chest expand as he took another deep breath.

Tears forced themselves into the corners of her eyes, but she blinked them back. This was *not* home, no matter what she felt. Jace was *not* the man for her, no matter how much her heart told her otherwise. They were *not* meant to be together just because cruel fate had thrown them together. This was simply an idyll. They would enjoy each other, then go about their business.

Jace tilted his head and kissed the slope of her shoulder. "You smell good."

She pulled away and looked up at him. "I smell like soap."

He grinned. "Good soap. From now on, whenever I smell this brand, I'll think of you."

One long nail gave in to temptation and outlined the dimple in his cheek. "Right," she said dryly, but knew her voice sounded breathless. "You don't even know what brand it is."

Jace chuckled. "You can bet I'll find out, sweets." He trailed his hands around her hips to rest on each side and pulled her to him. "And part of that smell is you. Just you." He nuzzled her neck, spreading kisses over the soft dampness of her skin, leaving tingles everywhere his lips touched.

Her breath caught in her throat.

The walk from bath to bed was short, the lovemaking that followed long and tender. It wasn't until the sun disappeared from the windows that Alicia realized they'd been preoccupied for hours.

Her hands on his chest and her chin resting on her hands, she lay on top of him and examined the strength of his jaw. It was the nicest one she'd ever seen—not that she'd ever paid much attention before. His hand was leisurely stroking her back and arms.

"It's dark," she commented lazily.

"It has been for a while," Jace answered, not stopping his exploration of the white skin beneath his palm.

"Really? Isn't it time you fed me?" Alicia asked, her fingernail drifting along his jaw, detouring by an ear.

"Spiritually or physically?"

"Physically," she replied quickly, unwilling to delve any further into her own feelings.

"What do you feel like eating?" Jace wrapped a thick strand of her hair around his fingers.

They'd never really confronted the problem other couples went through during the mating game. If you were in Mexico, it was enough to find a good restaurant. Styles and types weren't an issue. "Chinese?"

Jace grinned. "Hunan? Mandarin? Cantonese?"

She decided to take a chance and see if he was really as knowledgeable as he presented himself. Besides, she loved to banter with him. "Are there any Vietnamese restaurants in Chicago?"

"Yes, but I haven't tried them," he answered. "Would you like to?" His fingers trailed down her spine. "We could scour the countryside looking for the perfect restaurant. All night if necessary. Anything that pleases you."

"Are you adventurous or are you waiting for me to turn down the offer?"

His hand stilled its wandering. His gaze was on her and she could feel the heat. "When it comes to saying one thing and meaning another, I don't play games. Do you want me to learn?"

"No." Her voice was a whisper as she looked back at him. She hadn't expected him to invite confrontation. From what she'd known about him and seen in his file, she'd expected him to be suave and controlled enough to circumvent any argument. Apparently she was wrong. "But I do want you to feed me."

He grinned. "Let's go."

"Right," she said, not moving. Suddenly she was reluctant to pull away.

The air-conditioning whirred on and a cool wind blew across her skin. It didn't matter. He radiated body heat, keeping her as warm as a blanket. She stroked his chest through the fine material of his shirt and saw him glance down and watch her fingers at play. Desire swamped her.

"In a minute." Her voice was a whisper filled with need, she knew.

Jace felt his eyes burn with the same need. With a groan he covered her lips with his own and once more transported them to another place, another time. Before losing himself completely he wondered how love—real love—could be any different.

8

WITHIN TWENTY-FOUR HOURS, the work load of the Bartholomew building renovation and redecoration doubled. As instructed, Alicia's secretary in San Francisco mailed all the samples of tiles, fabrics, carpets and colors that Alicia thought she might need. As usual, half the factories were running behind schedules, and half the products Alicia checked on weren't available.

Kendall came in early every morning and they were hard at work by 8:00 a.m. Every once in a while, Alicia's gaze would wander toward the door that Jace had left through just after dawn. Once more she felt the draw he exerted over her. Then she gave herself a mental shake and got back to work again.

She saw Kendall stare at her from time to time, then burrow back into her own work. All day long they pored over the floor-by-floor blueprints, then explored the present physical layout, comparing the two before studying the catalogs and determining which table, chair, cabinet, side table and file cabinet would go where.

By six or seven at night, Alicia had sent Kendall home. The moment her secretary left, Jace appeared at her door. Obviously someone was watching them and telling Jace when she was alone. It wasn't a good feeling. In fact it was an invasion of privacy. She began looking over her shoulder.

But once Jace held her in his arms, she refused to dwell on such problems. Their time together was too precious to waste looking for ghosts or shadows. She needed his arms, his comforting presence.

But one week into the project, tired and irritated at the thought of someone watching her and needing to blow off nervous steam, Alicia met him at the door as he walked into the apartment.

His brows rose as he came toward her, but he was apparently undaunted by her aggressive, hands-on-hips stance. Without hesitation his hands circled her waist and pulled her into his arms. Then he covered her mouth with his. Once he'd gotten the kiss he wanted, he stepped back.

"What's wrong?"

"How do you know my every move?"

He walked to the bar and poured himself a drink. "I don't."

"Well, you know enough to know when Kendall leaves."

"The security guard tells me that. He sees Kendall leave and calls me."

"At your request?"

His brows rose again. "Of course, at my request. We have seven hundred employees in the building. I don't want to know when everyone leaves, just when Kendall finishes her work for the day. Besides, Kendall leaves so much later than the regular staff that I want the security guard to be aware and watch out for her."

She wanted to remain angry, wanted to tell him to stop having her watched. But his explanation forced her to reevaluate. He wasn't having her watched, he was having Kendall's exit accounted for. That was his right.

She sighed. "You're frustrating as hell. You know that, don't you?"

He smiled, walked back to her and placed a kiss upon her forehead. "I'll settle for that for now. Any emotion out of you is better than none."

"Doesn't your security guard wonder why you need to know?"

"Certainly. I told him that she was working with you and I needed to know when the top floor was empty of personnel."

"You have an answer for everything."

"No. I have a few good answers I give over and over again." He grinned, then ducked, just before she hit him with a couch pillow. Their laughter seemed to fill the corners of the room the sun had already deserted. Suddenly warmth was everywhere. Alicia refused to believe that most of it came from her heart.

But when his arms circled her waist once again and pulled her to his own lean form, she heard a voice whisper, *Fool!* For the moment she ignored it.

But that night the word returned to haunt her sleep.

THE PACE OF WORK speeded up. For Alicia, one day ran into another, separated only by the weekends when she and Jace relaxed, padding around the secluded suite in jeans and bare feet. Their conversations, however, were always and only about business. Thoughts and dreams were mentioned in passing, but she could tell he was as leery as she was about discussing the future or making any noises that had a sound of permanence.

Frightened though she was by that word, Jace seemed to be even more so. When she thought of it, her spirits drooped. They were quite a pair—two people who wouldn't even try to be together.

She promised herself not to think of that. It was too depressing. Instead she immersed herself in work, pretending that they would always be together. She'd cope with the alternatives later, after she left here. She'd have the rest of her life for regrets.

She was standing with Kendall in the center of the lobby, despairing over the tall, cathedral-type windows, when she suddenly realized that the paneling had never been a part of the original decor. The windows were too recessed and the paneling wrapped around them already emphasized that point.

That had already struck Alicia as odd and she had been thinking about it for some time—especially since the architect hadn't finalized his plans for the lobby. But the first clue that she was about to make a major discovery came when she absently measured off the distance of the outside wall from the bank of elevators and came up a foot short of the figure on the blueprint. Calculating more precisely she measured again, with Kendall checking her figures.

Although she managed to remain calm on the outside, an inner excitement was growing. Those ugly, twenty-four-foot-high paneled walls were not the originals. They were a cover-up, obviously put there in a later renovation. And they stood at least a foot away from the original surface.

Ignoring the passing people, she stared hard at the offending wood. Why? Having always hated paneling of every kind, she wondered who would have put up something as ugly as this, and why.

Kendall's research revealed that the building had been most recently renovated sometime in the late forties, soon after the war. The articles didn't mention what the lobby had looked like before, but did say that benches and other seating used to occupy some of the floor space.

Alicia knew that many commercial buildings had been renovated after World War II because the men had come home and needed jobs. Building owners could get good, cheap labor and help the economy at the same time. This was obviously one of those buildings.

With renewed determination Alicia picked up a screwdriver, sat down and began splintering the wood away from the gray marble floor. Years of wet-mopping the area had made the paneling easy prey. Her heartbeat quickened as she made a hole large enough to fit her hand through.

First she touched more marble flooring, then the real wall. Her excitement grew and she grinned at Kendall. "This surface is covering about six inches of marble. I can feel the real wall on the other side."

Kendall bent down and tried to peer through. "Now what?"

Alicia picked up the screwdriver again. "We make a hole big enough to see what I'm feeling."

"What if Bartholomew Corporation doesn't want this wall removed? We'll have a big hole to repair." Kendall was clearly worried.

Alicia jumped and saw Kendall do the same as a deep male voice spoke behind them. "Then we'll have to get out the whip and beat you both for destruction of private property," Cam stated emphatically.

A giggle rose to Alicia's lips. "More than your property would be destroyed with an action like that!" she exclaimed, standing to shake hands. No matter how much of a rake Cam was, he was also fun to be around. "How are you doing, Cam? And what are you doing here?"

"I'm doing fine, Alicia." He grinned. "And how are you and your lovely building inspector doing? Better still, *what* are you doing?" Despite addressing her, he only had eyes for Kendall, Alicia noted.

"I'm going to be here for a week or so, Alicia. Do you think you can put up with seeing me roam around this old building while you're slaving away?"

"You can keep Jace company."

"I understand he's already 'keeping' company with a certain person."

Alicia felt her skin warm to a blush. The amount of time she and Jace spent together was obviously known to Cam, and perhaps to the rest of his family as well.

"Did I say something wrong?" Cam asked innocently. His grin was even more deadly than the twinkle in his eyes, Alicia thought.

"Of course not," she replied quickly, moving toward the elevators. She sent Kendall a thankful glance as her secretary engaged Cam in a conversation about the difference in the weather patterns between New York and Chicago. Alicia knew it was silly, but she'd never given a thought to the probability that the rest of the world would find out about her affair with Jace. Of course, a few in the office no doubt knew. But his family? The entire office? Suddenly she felt exposed. Vulnerable.

Her thoughts grew into wishes. She wished Jace felt strong enough about their relationship to commit himself to it. As soon as the wish was born, she stifled it. That could only lead to pain and heartache. She would have enough of that once she returned to San Francisco—she didn't need any right now.

Kendall and Cam's voices murmured around her, but she didn't take in the words. When the elevator stopped, she stepped out on Jace's office floor as if she did it all the time. But the truth was, Alicia had kept away from his territory so no one would have an occasion to gossip—an effort she was now aware had been made in vain.

When they reached the outer office, Virginia glanced up from the file folders piled on her desk and smiled. If Alicia hadn't known better, she'd have sworn that the executive secretary had a crush on Cam.

"It's about time," Virginia said in a businesslike tone, but her smile softened the words.

Cam grinned, leaning over the desk to place a kiss upon her cheek. "I know. I stayed away as long as I could, Ginny, my sweet. But I missed you too much to be in exile forever. I decided to brave your husband's wrath and sneak in to see you."

"The golden tongue," she said reprovingly, but Alicia knew she was pleased by his teasing.

Cam sighed. "I speak words of love and she punctures my ego."

Kendall giggled.

But when Jace walked into the reception area, all Alicia's thoughts of Cam, Kendall or of golden tongues disappeared. Dressed in an expensive dark gray suit, he had chosen a maroon Hermès tie to set it off. His gaze fixed on her immediately, and the light in his blue eyes made her feel warm all over.

Cam's voice interrupted their silent communication. After a brotherly hug, Jace invited them all into the office. Kendall hesitated, apparently unsure as to what was proper. Alicia took her arm and herded her in with the rest of them. After all, if she was going to spend time with both men, so should her secretary.

Cam might not say anything else of a personal nature if a stranger was present.

Brotherly greetings and inquiries over, Jace looked again at Alicia, then at Kendall. He raised his brows as he realized that Alicia carried a screwdriver and several long, thick splinters of paneling. The reason they were in his office had clearly nothing to do with Cam's arrival. "Something going on?"

"Yes," Alicia began, unable to suppress the excitement of her find as she spoke. "The ugly lobby paneling is a front. I want to tear away a full section and find out what it's covering."

Jace was completely confused. "Say that again?"

Cam laughed. "I came across these two women poking holes in the paneling. Apparently it's a false wall, hiding six inches—" he glanced at Kendall and Alicia for confirmation "—six inches of space. The original wall is covered by that stuff."

Jace glanced at his watch. "It's almost quitting time. Do you want to wait until the offices have closed? Then I'll help you tear away a section."

Excitement fairly bubbled now inside Alicia. "Yes, but Kendall needs to get home."

She saw her secretary's eyes widen. "Are you kidding? I'm not leaving until I find out what's behind there! This is like hunting for a buried treasure. I want to know what we found."

"A woman after my own heart," Cam commented.

"I don't think so," Kendall said quietly but firmly, surprising Alicia with her outspokenness. She stared at Kendall and saw her assistant turn five shades of red, just as she herself had done earlier.

Jace broke the spell by offering drinks all around. He mixed and Alicia served. For just a moment Alicia felt as if she and Jace were a couple entertaining. It was a wonderful feeling of belonging, but it was only temporary, she reminded herself.

As she sipped at her soft drink and listened to the conversation, she couldn't take her eyes from Jace at his desk. Papers were stacked neatly in its center, as were the closed files to one side. He was devastatingly handsome, independently thorough and organizationally neat. Not a bad combination.

An hour passed. No matter how patient Alicia forced herself to be, her project was too exciting and her curiosity too aroused for her to sit still for long. Excusing herself, she went back up to her suite and found the hammer she'd seen in the kitchen cabinet earlier. Beside it lay a gardener's glove. She grabbed it, too.

They must have realized how impatient she was, she thought, for when she returned, they were already walking toward the elevator.

Jace smiled and let his hand drift to her waist as they waited. For a minute she forgot what she was waiting for. "Are you ready?" he inquired.

She nodded and down they went.

Two women from the offices sat on a concrete bench just inside the lobby, chatting while they waited for their rides. A heavyset security guard stood by the desk at the entrance, reading a newspaper.

Alicia made a beeline for the paneling they had splintered earlier. As she squatted into position, Jace took the hammer away from her and sat down, too.

"You'll get your suit dirty," she protested in a low voice.

"Then I'll have to remove it," he answered with a knowing gleam in his eye that promised she would participate in that effort. He turned to the task at hand.

The very thought almost made her lose track of what they were doing. First of all Jace used the claw end of the hammer to break away more of the wood. Chunks fell to the floor. He worked diligently until the hole was almost as large as his seated form.

Impatient to see something, Alicia stilled his hands and stuck her head inside the hole. It took a moment for her eyes to adjust to the dimness within. The wood framing the windows allowed a small amount of light to enter. She stared up, her heart thumping heavily as she realized what she was looking at.

"Good grief!" she muttered.

"What is it?" Jace tugged at her hand. "What do you see?"

By the time she pulled her head out of the hole, she was certain. "I'm not sure who did it, but there's a mural on this wall."

"On this wall," he repeated slowly. "Do you think it might be on the other paneled walls, too?"

"Who knows?" she asked in return. "But I know it's on this one."

"Who's the artist?" Kendall asked, bending in her turn.

Alicia's excitement at her find was high. "I don't know, but I want the maintenance man down here in the morning. He can cut a doorway and we'll be able to decide what to do."

Jace stood, then extended a hand to help Alicia. "What kind of decisions?"

"Decisions like, is it a famous artist or a piece of junk? Is it a good mural, or does it look like one hastily painted on the wall of an Italian restaurant in downtown New York?"

Kendall caught on quickly. "Do we expose it and let the style and colors dictate the decor of the rest of the lobby, or should we cover it up with a lighter wall form?"

Alicia gave her a smile. "And if we do, we need to work with the architects. They need to know as soon as possible."

Jace stared at the two women, then walked toward the security guard. After a whispered consultation, he returned. "Let's all get a bite to eat. I've arranged it so that by the time we return, the maintenance man will have carved out a healthy chunk of the wood. We won't have to wait until tomorrow."

Before anyone could argue, he and Cam had Alicia and Kendall by the arm and were leading them toward the front door, where Jace knew his car and driver waited.

Cam said something to Kendall and the younger woman giggled. It was a nice sound, one that reminded Alicia of a time when fun had been the rule of the day instead of something that came her way only occasionally. She stole a glance at Jace, whose expression was as stern and determined as if he were rehearsing for a board meeting.

It was time to tease him out of his solemn mood and change that dark, strong and brooding expression to something lighter. "It was so nice of you to help with this project."

"It's my building."

"I know, but you could have insisted we leave it until morning. Then I would have had to try to persuade you differently by using all my feminine wiles to steal away your decision-making processes."

"You're not Delilah," he finally murmured. "You don't have a pair of shears."

"Samson and Delilah?" she asked, realizing how far off the mark she was. "I forgot."

Before he could answer, Cam and Kendall slipped into the large car and Jace and Alicia joined them.

"I wonder what the ordinary people are doing," Kendall said on a sigh, stretching out in the seat. It was clear that she wasn't sophisticated enough to pretend she didn't revel in the moment. In fact, she looked absolutely pleased with herself and with life.

"Probably the same thing we are," Cam replied. "Trying to get through heavy traffic. Wondering what they're going to have for dinner. Trying to guess what's on TV."

"And what are we going to have for dinner?" Alicia asked.

"Ribs," both men stated with such utter certainty that Alicia realized there was more to their answer than just a taste for the food. Preplanning had gone into this.

"I knew that," Kendall told her. "I've heard about them both always having ribs the first night that Mr. Bartholomew comes into town. It's been going on for some time, hasn't it?"

"Five years," Cam confirmed. "There's nothing better than ribs with the best greasy barbecue sauce in the world. And coleslaw that looks as if it's been sitting out overnight, yet is so tasty it cuts the grease with a film of its own."

Kendall made a face. "Ugh."

Alicia's stomach lurched. She swallowed hard.

"It's great," Jace said and grinned. "We know the best greasy-rib place in town."

Alicia's stomach turned over. She placed a hand at her waist. Continuing to hold her stomach and press, she allowed the conversation to drift around her.

This was the third time in a week that she'd been queasy. Normally she had a stomach lined with cast iron, but not lately. She counted the time since her last period and realized with a shock it had been a little over five weeks.

Time flies when you're having fun.

Fear and excitement warred within her. Her ears buzzed with quickened, heated blood. From somewhere deep inside came the answer. She was pregnant. *She was pregnant!* She knew it without a shadow of a doubt. Despite the queasiness, she found herself smiling.

"Please, no barbecue tonight," she requested, breaking into the conversation. She didn't care what plans the brothers had made; there was no reason good enough for her to upset her baby by throwing up.

Alicia saw the group look at her, startled. It was suddenly so quiet that she could hear the car engine purr. Cam glanced at Kendall, then back to Alicia. "You don't like barbecue?"

Alicia grinned, but before she could answer, Jace answered for her. "It's not un-American not to like barbecue, Cam. We'll have it at lunch tomorrow."

Kendall leaned over. "What do you feel like having?"

"Italian?" Alicia was asking her stomach more than gauging the reaction of the others. When it didn't lurch at the thought, she let her grin grow wide. "Italian," she repeated.

Without consulting anyone, Jace leaned forward and spoke to the driver through the glass partition. The car changed direction and headed toward another part of the city.

"Northern Italian, with all those creamy sauces," Alicia said dreamily. Her thoughts were now so inner-focused that she hardly paid attention to the conversation that began again around her.

Another silence. Jace's hand rested on her shoulder. His other hand gently touched her knee. "Are you all right?" he asked in a low voice, his tone filled with concern.

Alicia wondered what he would say if she told him the truth. *I'm pregnant, and you're the father.* Somehow she didn't think he'd be too thrilled. That hurt, but not enough to spoil her joy. She covered his hand with her own.

"I'm fine," she said. "I'm just not a fan of barbecue. Not tonight." She leaned closer to his ear, breathing in his spicy after-shave. Jace was a wonderful man and if he would let himself, he'd be a marvelous father. She'd seen a side of him that most people never saw, and knew his vulnerabilities and strengths. But she also knew that he was younger than she was, and that he was not going to change enough to be good husband or father material. She doubted he would ever be.

A sadness permeated the wreath of happiness that had circled Alicia since she'd made her discovery. Knowing she couldn't allow Jace to guess the source of either emotion, she kept her smile in place.

Cam and Kendall were arguing the merits of the creamy northern sauces versus the thick, rich tomato sauces of southern Italian cooking when the driver pulled up to a restaurant in the heart of the city. A canopied entrance announced that the restaurant had originated in Milan.

Alicia reflected that she should have known that Jace's knowledge of restaurants would be excellent.

The sauce was the lightest and creamiest she'd ever eaten. Crisp salad and thick, hot bread began the meal. The homemade ravioli stuffed with healthy spinach was melt-in-your-mouth delicious. Not wanting to draw attention to herself, she didn't refuse wine, but nursed one glass all through dinner. Afterward she ordered decaffeinated coffee.

Jace leaned toward her. "Is your stomach still upset?"

"No, why?"

"I just wondered," he murmured before finishing the last of his wine.

But she couldn't leave it at that. "What made you think I had an upset stomach?"

He studied her face before speaking again. "Little things like swallowing several times before you turned down our original plans. Then you held your stomach. Then—" his voice dropped "—then you pasted a smile on your face that told me you were in pain."

She felt trapped by his gaze and finally cast her eyes downward. His eyes were too direct, too all-seeing. His comments should have been warning enough. Instead she'd been so wrapped up in her own excitement that she hadn't disguised the obvious signs of something gone awry.

"I was feeling queasy earlier," she said slowly, her mind reviewing other excuses and discarding them. "I guess I got so excited about our discovery this afternoon, my stomach was upset."

Jace leaned back, his eyes still on her. He nodded and seemed to accept her excuse. "What do you think we'll find this evening when we get back?" he asked, changing the subject.

"I have no idea," she answered candidly, relieved that the subject of her stomach was forgotten. Perhaps she'd answered more honestly than she cared to admit. With the discovery of the fake wall and the realization that she was carrying a baby—Jace's baby—it might have all been hard on her stomach. At least it wasn't a direct lie.

Just in case, she crossed her fingers.

Two hours later and with Cam and Kendall's debate on the economy still in progress, they left the restaurant to return to the Bartholomew Building.

Alicia's heart, already thumping hard, began pounding. Jace's arm was around her shoulders, one finger resting on the hollow of her throat. "Your pulse is racing."

"I'm excited," she told him, unwilling to admit how deeply his touch affected her. "I haven't been happy with any of my plans for the lobby, and from the looks of the architect's renderings, they're not one hundred percent pleased with their efforts, either."

Jace's hand covered hers. All through the drive back, Alicia stared out the window at the city beyond. She felt overwhelmed by a myriad of emotions. Having Jace seated beside her didn't seem to help, either. When he was close, all her senses were attuned to him, so that she could not think coolly and rationally.

His thumb gently massaged her palm. A warmth stole through her blood, making tense muscles relax. By the time the limo stopped in front of the building, Alicia had calmed considerably. Her happiness over the baby was still present, and the hand held in Jace's also gave comfort, allowing her to postpone worries about the future.

The security guard was waiting for them. He approached Jace as they walked across the lobby to where the maintenance man stood, a small electric saw in hand.

"An' I told Joe here to make a space as big as a doorway, but to make sure that he didn't do nothing to the wall behind it. And he did that, and guess what he found?"

Alicia stopped walking and turned toward the guard, her thoughts leaping from one possibility to another. "What?" she asked.

"A picture." The guard rocked on his heels. "A picture as big as the wall."

"A mural?"

The workman with the saw joined them. "Yea, that's it. A mural." He jerked his head toward the large orange flashlight sitting on the floor. "You can see it with my light."

Alicia picked up the light and, standing at the newly sawed entrance, she aimed the beam at the wall. Brilliant oranges, pinks, muted peaches and blues, all jumbled together, reached at least thirty feet high.

She tried to see how far to each side the mural went, but it was too dark. In the morning, she thought, she'd be able to see it with the advantage of daylight. It would be her first project.

When she stepped back, Jace's arms circled her waist and he rested his hands just below. Right on top of the baby. She closed her eyes and smiled. "You're excited?" he whispered into her ear.

She nodded. Jace might not love her, but he was demonstrative enough to show affection in public. And she loved that about him. "Aren't you?"

"Yes." His voice dropped an octave. "Very."

"Some people can stand and stare at a mural all night, but others need sleep," Cam told them. "I'm taking Kendall home and crashing at your apartment, Jace. See you later." He walked Kendall toward the door, resting his hand on the lower part of her back.

Kendall looked as if she were warring with both fear and excitement. Alicia hoped she wouldn't get hurt.

Then she turned, stared at Jace and realized she had no room to worry about Kendall. She was up to her nose in alligators and didn't have time to fret about someone else's mess.

9

WHEN ALICIA opened her eyes the next morning, she found Jace curled intimately around her, one hand cupping a breast. Warm breath caressed her neck. Blinking for a second, she lay still, afraid to wake Jace in case he turned away before she was ready.

She couldn't admit it to him, but Alicia reveled in his nearness—looked forward to waking in his arms every morning. It was unbelievable to her that she had grown to the age of thirty-six before she realized what some women meant when they said they couldn't sleep alone. She was becoming addicted—needed his presence like she needed to eat or sleep. But Jace wasn't interested in any relationship that smacked of commitment.

The baby. The thought came out of the blue and brought her fully awake. Panic at the idea that Jace might feel subtle differences in her body made her move. Carefully easing herself from his grasp, she stepped into the bathroom and closed the door before running icy water to rinse her face and cool her pulse. Then she caught sight of herself in the mirror.

She leaned forward and stared at the skin around her eyes and mouth. Unless one looked carefully, no one would notice the fine lines that were beginning to make their home there. But she saw them plain and clear. As the years passed, they would embed themselves even deeper and turn into wrinkles. Jace was interested in her for more than her looks, but how would he really feel about her when Mother Nature began to exact her toll?

Well, at least she was going to have a child of her own to raise and cherish.

That made life—and wrinkles—worth tolerating.

"Alicia?" Jace's voice drifted through the door, wrapping her in a soft, warm cocoon of sound.

"I'll be right there," she called, reaching for a toothbrush. According to her schedule, she had another two weeks before she had to leave for San Francisco. She was going to make the best of it and be with Jace as much as possible. Once she left, she'd never see him again. There was no alternative.

WHEN ALICIA LEFT the warmth of their bed and silently padded to the bathroom, Jace felt as if she was leaving him—for good. He allowed her to believe he was still asleep because that was what she obviously wanted. But he was instantly lonely. In the short time since they'd been lovers, he'd come to depend upon her presence, even in sleep. Dining without her conversation was like eating dry documents. Drinking without her laughter was like sipping sawdust. Going to bed without her curled next to him was like sleeping on nails. He hated feeling dependent, but loved the invisible connection that existed between them. Although he'd heard others talk of it, he'd never experienced it before. This wasn't like being married or otherwise closely tied to someone. It was a new feeling, one he'd sought all his life.

It's a matter of joint commitment. You've never committed yourself to anyone before, the voice in his head told him.

But he knew better. He'd committed his heart and soul to his daughter. To this day he missed her. She was a part of him, a person who would carry on where he left off. She was everything to him. His daughter, however, refused to have anything to do with him—thanks to her mother.

That's not true and you know it. That's an excuse you've been using all this time. An excuse that allowed him to remember better times without having to expend any energy on doing something to change things. As long as he blamed his ex-wife, the relationship with Meagan was out of his hands.

Jace turned over, not liking the path his thoughts were taking. He didn't want to think of the past, but of the present. Of Alicia.

When he called her name, he was actually saying a prayer. He didn't want her to leave. *Ever.* But short of telling her that, he didn't know how to make her do it. Besides, she had this crazy thing about his age, continually teasing him about the four-year difference between them. It was all a pile of trash as far as he was concerned. He just wasn't sure if she realized that.

All thoughts fled as she came out of the bathroom and walked toward the bed. Naked, with her blond hair curling around her face and shoulders, she looked like a golden angel. He hardened with desire. As she slipped into bed, her smile lighted up the room.

He held out his arms and she slid into his embrace. "You're beautiful," he murmured, taking a deep breath and inhaling the scent of her.

"Mmm," she purred, pressing her body against him, restlessness apparent in her movements as she cuddled closer.

"I love the way your body fits mine."

"Mmm," she said again. "I thought it was the other way around."

"And the way you feel when you rub against me— never mind the way you taste." He dipped his head and took one rosy nipple into his mouth, sucking gently.

Her body arched to his lips, her answer turning into a moan. Turning her onto her back, Jace let his hands roam the softness of her hips and thighs, the light roundness of her belly, the silkiness of her hair. His palm lightly rubbed against the juncture of her thighs. Alicia moved against his hand, telling him she was as ready for loving as he was.

His touch grew lighter, sensitizing her even more. Then suddenly she pulled out of his grasp and pinned him to the mattress.

She looked down at him, a brilliance in her eyes telling him to follow rather than lead. "Do you have something else in mind?" she asked, straddling his hips.

"No."

"You didn't think you'd torture me until I couldn't see straight?"

"No." It was a lie and she knew it.

She allowed him to slip into her, but when he tried to thrust, held him back.

Her head bent closer to his. Her lips parted, her warm breath caressing his jaw. "No? Why was it that I felt as if you were seeing how long you could hold out while making me pay for my own desires?"

Jace grinned ferociously, but allowed her to keep his hands at his shoulders. "Because I was?"

She nodded, her lips brushing his. "I thought so," she murmured. "You're a big tease. What you didn't real-ize was that what's good for the goose is also good for the gander."

His head was swimming with emotions, making him breathless, making him want to hold her forever. With a light twist, his hands were free and resting on her hips.

Alicia sat up in surprise, then closed her eyes and rocked back and forth, following his movements. He loved watching her facial expressions as he made love to her. She was so open, so wonderfully guileless—an aphrodisiac in herself.

"Come forward," he whispered and she did as he asked. Lifting his head, he took one pebbled nipple into his mouth. Their rocking increased. His heart was beating so strongly that he thought it would pound its way through his ribs. Suddenly he felt her tighten around him. Her eyes closed, her body remained suspended in his hands.

He felt his own explosion like a burst of energy. Holding tightly to her, he drifted slowly back to reality with Alicia still in his arms. A strand of her hair grazed his chest and neck, and he leaned to one side and kissed her cheek.

"Wonderful," he murmured with a sigh.

"Lovely," she agreed in a whisper.

"Perfect."

"Perfect."

His arms tightened, unwilling to relinquish this woman—to be alone again. Still feeling languid in the aftermath of making love, Jace found it hard to believe that he didn't want to jump from the sack and run like hell. That was how he had usually felt. In fact, that was what he'd usually *done*. He wasn't proud of it, but there it was.

But with Alicia, he wanted to remain a part of her as long as he could. *Forever,* if possible.

Warning bells went off in his head. They were so loud he was surprised that Alicia couldn't hear them. The only way to stop them ringing was to free himself from the woman who had set them going.

He did just that, rolling away and standing by the side of the bed.

Alicia opened her eyes and stared at him in the early-morning silence. He could see surprise, then hurt invade those beautiful eyes, but couldn't do anything about it. She needed more from him than he could give. If he'd had more to give at that moment, he would have done so. His body responded before his mind and made a move toward her. Then he pulled back and strode to the bathroom, closing the door firmly behind him; temptation was on the other side.

He wanted to laugh, then to cry.

Temptation always exacted a heavy price. And for the first time in his life, he wasn't sure what the price was for giving in to it. He also didn't give a damn.

Angry with his old fears, he opened the door and stepped out, wanting to follow his first impulse and take Alicia back into his arms and tell her how much he cared.

The bed was empty.

ALICIA MARCHED around the kitchen as she made a pot of strong coffee. She almost threw the canister back against the wall. She spilled water as she poured it too quickly into the back of the brewer. She flipped the switch with a forceful push. Then she had nothing else to do. Arms folded belligerently, she leaned against the counter and glared at the humming refrigerator.

Okay. She got the point. She wasn't a necessity in Jace's life. She was *wanted* or she wouldn't be in his arms every night, but if she was *needed*, she'd be in his life during the day, too. Apparently, a good mind and great career weren't things he looked for in a female. Neither was love.

She heard the shower start and knew that Jace was getting ready for work.

In spite of Alicia's anger, tears welled into her eyes. Damn him!

Anyone else's rejection wouldn't hurt half as much as Jace's. She wasn't involved with anyone else. He was the one she loved, even though she'd known from the beginning that it was hopeless. She hadn't been forced into this position; she'd willingly put herself here. All the warning signs had been out, but she'd ignored them. It was her fault for rationalizing the danger.

Now she was pregnant. It was a small piece of heaven in the hell she'd created. But she couldn't breathe a word about it, or he'd probably kick her out on her ear. Now that she had to prepare for having another mouth to feed, she'd better save every dime she could. And this job came with a hefty price tag.

Jace walked into the kitchen, rubbing his wet hair with a forest-green towel. An identical towel was slung low around his hips, looking as if it stayed there by magic or determination. She wasn't sure which.

"What do you want?" Alicia asked, daring him to say one tender word. After walking away from her, he could darn well roast on a spit before she would ever let him know she responded to him.

His eyes widened. He looked around the kitchen as if seeking gremlins, then glanced at her. "Coffee?"

She bowed with a flourish. "Be my guest."

Still he didn't move. "Aren't you having any?"

Actually, the smell of the brew was making her stomach queasy. But she would certainly not whisper a word of that to him. She nodded regally. "When I'm ready."

Jace walked to the kitchen cabinet, pulling a towel over one broad shoulder. "Would you like me to pour you some?"

"No, thank you," she said stiffly. Her pulse rate increased as she watched his fluid movements.

"Can I interest you in a big breakfast?" he asked as he poured himself a cup and mimicked Alicia's stance on the other side of the kitchen. "Eggs, bacon, pancakes?"

Alicia swallowed. "No, thank you."

"How about me?"

What was he talking about? "Pardon me?"

"Would you like to go to bed with me again?" He stared at her, clearly willing her—no—demanding that she answer. She swallowed again, but this time because of the lie she was about to utter. "No, thank you."

Jace stared at her a moment more. Without saying another word, he pushed away from the counter and walked back into the living area.

Alicia let out her breath. She would have loved to have flown into the comfort of his arms. But it wouldn't have worked. It would never work.

Whether she wanted to admit it or not, it was time to call off this relationship and head back to the safety of San Francisco.

This time the tears spilled over.

KENDALL SHOWED UP late for work. The look on her face was a mixture of sheepishness and defiance. "I overslept."

Alicia nodded, returning her attention to the drawings in front of her. They were the blueprints of the lobby. "Happens to everyone."

"I don't normally do that."

Still Alicia didn't look up. "I agree." She heard Kendall stride around the office area, grabbing files and seeking the proper file cabinets to shove them into place.

Alicia waited as long as she could. Knowing the misery another woman was going through didn't lessen her own, but it did make things less lonely. "What did you think of Cam Bartholomew?" She glanced at her secretary.

Kendall stood still, her gaze rooted to the floor. "I thought he was wonderful and smooth and sincere and a liar."

"I agree with everything except the liar bit. To my knowledge, he's never been accused of that before."

Kendall looked at her, a question in her eyes. "You've known him for a long time?"

"Only by reputation. His older brother, Brad, married one of my friends. I met him for the first time three months ago."

"And what is his reputation?"

Alicia glanced back at the blueprints on the table in front of her. "Professional or personal?" she hedged.

Kendall's answer came quickly. "Both."

Sitting down, Alicia mentally debated how much to say. She hated to be the one to bear bad tidings, but if she were in Kendall's place she'd want to know what others said about a man who had the potential to hurt her. "He's an astute businessman. He's also a womanizer, if that word is still used. Cam seems to love women." She looked pointedly at her assistant. "All women."

Kendall's shoulders drooped. "That's what I thought."

Walking around the desk, Alicia placed an arm around Kendall in a comforting gesture. "It may be all talk."

"Thanks, but I think you and I know better."

Heavy at heart, Alicia returned to work. After making several phone calls about supplies she needed to complete the office floors, she finally felt ready to see the rest of the lobby wall.

Despite her mood, excitement mounted as the elevator took the two of them to the lobby. As the doors opened, her eyes darted to the wall in front of her. The maintenance man had sawed away still more of the dark paneling, and even from this distance she could see a portion of the mural. Slim, female feet clad in narrow wedged heels, painted in the Art Deco style.

Her pulse raced. She knew that style. She knew.... Striding up to the cutout section, Alicia picked up the workman's large flashlight from the floor and shone it onto the wall.

"It's an Erté," she whispered.

"Who's Erté?" Kendall whispered back.

Alicia flashed the light into the far corner, attempting to penetrate the darkness. She still couldn't see the whole mural, but the peaches, mauve, rich golds and blues told her she was right. "He was a Russian immigrant who studied in Paris, then came to America and worked for some of the greatest fashion magazines in the country. He was a wonderful artist, practically inventing Art Deco."

"And he did murals?"

"No. There was a rumor that he had wanted to, but no one ever thought he had. Until now."

Kendall's voice rose. "You mean, we have the only mural he ever painted?"

Her enthusiasm was catching. Alicia nodded. "It looks that way."

"What are we going to do with it?"

Smiling, Alicia gave the answer without a second's hesitation. "We're going to uncover it, authenticate it, then exploit it. All for the good of the Bartholomew Corporation and the average passerby."

For a moment, the realization that she would not be there to see the lobby in its completed glory was heartbreaking. Shaking off that feeling, she went on. "And we'll have to move quickly. I want this wall down by the end of the week."

Kendall began writing in her notebook. "All of it or just this part?"

"All of it. We don't know what's behind the rest of this ugly paneling. Who knows? There may be more surprises in store."

At lunchtime Alicia ordered sandwiches sent to her office. Now that she knew she was pregnant, she wanted to run and hide, afraid that Jace might discover her secret. It would be terrible, not only because he would be angry, but because it would signal the end of their relationship. She just wanted to do her job and get out of Chicago. The sooner the better, she kept telling herself, even though her heart felt as if it was breaking in two.

Every once in a while she'd pull herself up short. *Stop it!* she commanded silently. *Stop dwelling on what you cannot change and be thankful for your blessings!* Her stern talk didn't do much good. Her bruised heart still hurt.

By the time the late-afternoon sun began to disappear from the office window, she was exhausted. Reaching into her drawer, Alicia grabbed and gulped two vitamin Cs and an iron pill, then leaned back and closed her eyes.

The architect had done a wonderful job, so Alicia knew her work amounted to enhancing the personal areas with decor that matched the plans already set up. Her task would probably be completed in less than a week, with only the items she had had to back-order needing placement later.

But the lobby was hers to play with and would take longer. The architects had done exactly what Alicia had expected; they'd taken one look at the murals and asked her opinion.

"I want the paneled walls taken down, then I'll line up the floor covering and accents. The windows should be outlined in brass, the accent colors picked from the mural itself."

"Of course," Howard Ambrose had said, nodding his head up and down as if he were falling asleep.

The workers would begin taking down the paneling tonight and finish in two days. Alicia could conceivably be back in San Francisco by next week. Eight days.

She wanted to cry.

She did.

Later, as the building began to empty once more, Cam came to the office door and glanced around. Alicia was obviously not the object of his search.

"Looking for someone?" she asked, unable to keep a smile from her face. Bless Cam, at least he allowed her to come out of her misery for a moment.

"Is Kendall here?" Cam asked with a sheepish air.

Alicia shook her head. "She's on the fifth floor with one of the painters."

She saw Cam's eyes narrow as he looked at her more closely. "Your hair looks nice down. You don't wear it like that often."

"No," she admitted softly. "Do you notice what's different about every woman, Cam, or just an assorted few?" she teased.

He gave her one of the warm, boyish grins he was famous for. "I try to notice, but I don't always succeed. But with you I'd better notice. Jace might give me a quiz in the morning."

Pain constricted Alicia's heart. In another week she'd be gone. In two weeks Jace would probably not remember her name. "I doubt it."

Cam stepped inside the room and leaned against the wall. His manner was as open and friendly as ever, but Alicia was wary.

"Tell me, Alicia, are you taking my brother for an emotional roller-coaster ride or do you really care for him?"

"That's between your brother and myself, Cam."

He nodded in apparent agreement. "Normally you'd be right. But the fact is that when you're through playing with him, more than likely it'll be my job to pick up the pieces. You'll be gone."

Alicia tilted her head and gazed back. "What makes you think I'm playing? Your brother has a history of doing that, not me."

"Wasn't that what you were doing last night when you noticed you needed Italian food over barbecue? Testing him for a reaction? Seeing how high you could make him jump in front of others?"

She felt her eyes widen at the unfair accusation. Then she relaxed. Under the circumstances it was a reasonable assumption. But the truth was that even she had been surprised at how readily Jace had agreed to change restaurants. She didn't know what would have happened if he hadn't, however. She might have spent the evening with her arms around a porcelain bowl....

Alicia's grin wouldn't stay suppressed. Every time she thought about the baby, the grin popped out. "I wasn't playing power games, Cam. I really did have an upset stomach, and the thought of smelling barbecue sauce was too much."

Cam's arms were crossed over his broad chest, his head slightly bent. He stared at her as if he had an inner lie detector. "Really?"

"Really."

Her tone seemed to have convinced him, because he finally relaxed his stance. "I'm sorry. Are you feeling better now?"

"Somewhat." How could she admit that it was an indisposition that probably would remain for three months or so? She couldn't talk about that with anyone except her doctor.

"Would you and Jace like to join Kendall and me for dinner tonight? We're just going out for pizza."

"With her children?"

It was Cam's turn to look startled. "No, I don't think so. At least she didn't say anything about it."

"She has two youngsters, you know. It's tough raising children alone, Cam, but Kendall and a whole lot of other women are doing it." She knew she sounded as if she was lecturing, but had to do it.

Cam pushed away from the wall. "I know, Alicia. But I just asked her out for pizza. It's a date, not a marriage proposal."

"Don't hurt her," Alicia warned, then grinned. She had just assumed Cam's previous role. And Cam looked just as confident of his reasons as she was of hers.

"Don't worry. I'm just treating her to a few nights on the town. Everybody needs a little romance in their lives. Including mothers of little kids."

"And big kids who don't know the first meaning of the word mother," she added teasingly, only to see his expression suddenly grow rigid.

"Oh, I know the word," he replied. "And so does Jace. If there's one word we don't need a dissertation on, it's that one."

Alicia had forgotten about Jace and Cam's mother. Their experience with her had clearly marked the entire Bartholomew family. "I'm sorry."

Cam grinned. "Hey," he said, seeming to shrug off the thoughts that had changed his expression. "It's no big deal. I now forgive every woman everything and Jace won't forgive a woman for anything. He believes every single one has a bag of tricks she's just dying to use on him, so he tricks her first. All's fair in love and war."

Alicia felt her smile slip this time. Of course, Cam was right. His parents' legacy had helped to shape both him and his brothers, though each had reacted differently. What Cam or Brad would tolerate or even laugh at would anger Jace, and vice versa.

"Back in a few minutes," Cam murmured, moving toward the bathroom.

Alicia barely heard him, only glad he wasn't there to see her blush at the next thought. If or when Jace found out about her pregnancy, he'd never forgive her. There was no doubt that he'd believe she'd tried to trick him into a deeper relationship, one that he couldn't walk away from. Only he would.

She pressed suddenly weak hands against her belly, cradling the unborn child within and praying that nothing and no one would ever harm it by word or deed. After three days of believing herself pregnant, she was already fending off tigers; imaginary ones, but tigers just the same.

Nothing would be allowed to harm this pregnancy; neither bad food, ugly moods nor irate men who thought they were being trapped.

The object of her thoughts walked through the door. Without a word he moved behind her and extended his arms around her waist, pulling her toward the hardness of his body. His mouth teased one side of her neck, his touch igniting other thoughts, other moods. Jace swayed slowly back and forth, as if cradling her in his embrace. She loved it. She felt protected and cherished.

She covered his hands with her own and leaned back in his arms. She wouldn't allow harm to come to her baby, but until she left Chicago to go home, she would enjoy Jace and his touch. She was too much in love to do otherwise.

Besides, she had the rest of her life to be lonely.

10

IN THE EARLY HOURS of the morning, with Alicia firmly ensconced in his bed, Jace thought he'd come as close to heaven as he'd ever been.

Alicia stirred and he tightened his grip on the softness of her waist, unwilling to let her leave. He wouldn't admit it during the day, but Alicia was as necessary as sleep. With her by his side or in his arms, he could sleep as if he were a baby. Without her he spent the night tossing, turning and staring at the ceiling. It wasn't fair and it wasn't right, but it was fact.

He refused to delve into his feelings any further. It wasn't important to know *why* he felt that way, only to know what solutions worked with which problems. At least, that was how he usually felt. In fact it was how he'd felt at the beginning of this relationship, too. Somewhere along the line, those thoughts and feelings had changed. And as the decorating project drew to a close, he knew he'd have to think of something else to keep Alicia near him.

He was certain she didn't want to leave, either. He could tell she loved being with him. As if to underline that thought, he allowed his hand to drift down and stroke her lower belly. She sighed and moved closer. Alicia was still as slim as a reed, but in the last week or so she'd begun to put on a little weight. That should prove how content she was with him.

But then what? a tiny but persistent voice asked. *How long can you keep her here? How long do you expect this relationship to continue without a commitment?* He didn't have an answer.

He closed his eyes determinedly and willed himself back to sleep. He'd worry about it in the morning.

ALICIA WOKE later than usual and made a beeline for the bathroom. She could hear Jace in the kitchen and was relieved. Nausea first thing in the morning was not a pretty sight. Queasy stomachs seemed to have a mind of their own. Thank goodness, it didn't last long. Within fifteen minutes all was back to normal and she could smile again—or at least pretend to.

Jace greeted her as she came out of the steamy bathroom, a cup of coffee in his hand. He offered it to her and she had no choice but to take it. She held her breath, though. Coffee wasn't the right thing for a tense stomach.

Jace peered at her. "Are you all right?"

She smiled broadly. "I'm wonderful."

He grinned back. "I knew that."

When she felt a blush graze her cheeks, he laughed. Alicia ignored him and walked to the closet, pulling out a drab brown pair of slacks and a loose-fitting, khaki-colored cotton sweater.

"Nice," he said. He was still standing by the bathroom door.

She continued to ignore him, dressing quickly and with efficient movements. But her heart knew he was close. It kept beating in double time. His eyes seemed to burn a hole in her flesh before she covered it up.

"I want you to have lunch with me today."

Startled, she looked up. "Really? Why?"

His gaze was riveting. "I want to show you something."

She stopped what she was doing and stared at him. "What?"

"You'll see."

"A mystery?" she asked, finally slipping into her shoes. "That's not like you, Jace."

"You've classified me?"

Alicia started to brush her hair. With a deft hand, she twisted its length into a rope and pinned it to the top of her head. "Footloose, fancy-free and very up-front."

"I'm not sure I approve of that description."

"You don't have to," she said lightly. "It's my description."

He turned and rested his hands on her slim shoulders. An incredible warmth seeped into her. "Alicia," he began slowly, and her pulse quickened at the dark, rich timbre of his voice as the sound flowed through her body. He affected her in ways that no man had ever done. Although she loved him for arousing emotions that she didn't know she could have, she also resented her own reaction. "We've become closer than we meant to."

It bothered her to have him say it out loud. But it also meant he was willing to discuss things. That was more than he had done before. It sparked a tiny flame of hope. "I know."

"What do you think about it?"

"I don't know." At least her answer was honest. She really didn't know what to think about the pain she was in for when he walked away. In an earlier life she must have been a fool—and was paying for it now.

"What happens when this job is over? What will you do?"

"I'll go home," she said simply, pretending that her words hadn't hurt more than she'd thought possible.

"Forever?"

She took a deep, shaky breath and tried to smile. "Until the next job." There was no use in saying she wasn't going on the next job until after their baby was born. There was no use in saying anything.

If Jace had any idea she was pregnant, he would only turn from her in anger and disgust. Or he might fight for custody after the birth. She didn't know him well enough to be sure what he would do, but couldn't afford either reaction. Besides, either way she lost him.

His hands tightened. He bent forward and Alicia met him halfway, longing in her heart as well as her eyes.

Just as their lips brushed, the door from the hallway opened once more and Alicia heard Cam's deep voice as well as Kendall's as they walked into the living room. Alicia popped her eyes open.

Jace muttered an expletive under his breath and stepped back. "I'll go into the kitchen and pretend I was there all along," he muttered, giving her a consoling squeeze before turning away.

Alicia nodded. With a resoluteness she didn't know she was capable of, she turned and walked into the living-room and office area, doing her best to paint a bright smile onto her lips.

"Good morning."

Jace entered from the kitchen at the same time. "Good morning."

Both Cam and Kendall looked a little surprised, Alicia noted. She couldn't blame them; they had to feel a little like a wagon train under attack, with Jace at one end of the room and Alicia at the other. Cam at least had the advantage of knowing about their association. Kendall wasn't sure and Alicia had never clarified things with her.

Cam grinned. "Did you two just...begin your day?"

Jace frowned. "Yes."

Kendall began shuffling through the papers on top of Alicia's desk.

Alicia blushed and saw Cam's grin grow wider.

Jace positively scowled.

Kendall continued shuffling paperwork.

Alicia acknowledged defeat. Apparently it was written all over her that Jace and she had just gotten up. She joined Kendall in the paper chase.

In the awkward silence that followed, Jace and Cam muttered farewells and left. But as the elevator bell rang outside her room, she heard Cam's deep laughter. At lunchtime Virginia informed her that Jace was waiting downstairs in the car. Waving to Jace's secretary, Alicia tripped out the door to the elevator. Despite the inauspicious way the morning had begun, it had been a productive one. Her mind had clicked in all the right places and clacked when it was supposed to. And she saw "major progress," as Joy, her little secretary in San Francisco, would have said.

But she wouldn't think of that now, she told herself when she slipped into the sleek black limousine at the curb. Jace was leaning back, watching her every move, a smile tilting his full lips and making her pulse race. A pull-down tray in front of him held plates of artfully arranged sandwiches, as well as chips, pickles and glasses of iced tea.

Her mouth watered at the sight of pickles. "It looks wonderful," she murmured.

"Nice enough for a bribe?" Although his body seemed relaxed, his eyes glittered.

She leaned toward him, taking in yet again the masculine fragrance of his after-shave. It was light, but not overpowering. Tantalizing. Not just females could be provocative. "Any kind of payment you want." Her gaze fastened on his mouth and she watched with fascination the way he shaped the words he spoke.

Gently tugging on her hip, he pulled her closer, tangling his hand in the silkiness of her hair. "You know what I want," he growled before he claimed her lips in a kiss that ignited a fire that threatened to flame higher than the Bartholomew Building.

As the chauffeur pulled the car into traffic, Alicia barely felt the sway. Her arms circled Jace's neck, clinging to him for balance as well as to be close to him. His touch on her back was airy light, his lips were possessive, firm. Not domineering. A soft sigh escaped her as she pulled back and stared at him, sensing that stars were in her eyes.

"Was that a bribe or a reward?" she asked.

"Neither."

"I think it was a reward," Alicia decided, sprinkling light, teasing kisses upon his jaw.

Jace's breath was warm against her cheek. "I'm not even sure who was paying who," he said, stroking back a curl. The gesture sent shivers down her spine.

She rested her head against his chest and took another deep breath. "Does it matter?"

"No," he whispered. "Not at all." With obvious reluctance he pulled away from her and began unwrapping the plate of sandwiches.

She watched his hands. He had long, slender fingers that looked as if they should be playing the piano or clarinet. Beautiful, strong, masculine hands. Hands that touched and stroked her in places that she hadn't known were erogenous zones.

He caught her look and she saw a companion fire dance in his eyes. Visibly he forced himself to relax. Alicia leaned back and smiled.

The drive was as easygoing as the lunch. Alicia, determined to enjoy the trip, wherever they might be headed, caught him up in conversation and found herself discussing topics she hadn't thought of in years.

"Yes," she agreed, when he brought up the subject of recycling old houses. "The houses themselves were works of art, but their basic ingredients must be changed. Better insulation, treated wood and brick, and windows that reflect instead of absorb the sun's rays."

"A modern structure."

"An old-fashioned structure with modern improvements. Otherwise we might as well go back fifty years and pretend that the earth has an unlimited supply of everything. It's global suicide."

The car pulled up to a curb and for the first time, Alicia glanced out the window and realized they were somewhere in the country. Tall oaks and stunning maples pushed against each other at the side of the road. Houses were the old-fashioned, wooden two-storied kind that looked like movie sets from the thirties and forties.

Across the street was an apartment complex. It was unusual to see one here in a rural setting, but its design made it fit in perfectly, being both contemporary and Victorian.

"Like it?"

"I love it," she stated promptly. "Is it yours?"

He nodded. "Both in design and concept."

"Is this what we came to see?" Alicia was astonished.

He nodded again. His gaze remained with her. As she reached for the handle, he beat her to it, pushing the door open and allowing her out first. Giving the driver a sign to remain where he was, Jace placed one hand at the small of her back and led her toward the two-storied structure. Punching a number into a computer pad at the double doors, he waited for the buzz. It came quickly. With a deft movement, he pushed against one large door, then stood back for Alicia to enter.

Instead of being inside a building, as she had assumed she would be, she was in a courtyard. A very large, very unusual courtyard. Rectangular in shape, it looked almost as big as a football field. The yard was divided into squares, some holding a vegetable garden, others a play area or benches. The building on both sides was large enough for three stories of apartments. But the wing directly across from her had only two stories. Its windows were larger, the doors taller and wider.

"It's much bigger than it looks from the outside," Alicia murmured.

"I hope so," Jace answered. "I tried to scale it down. Even the parking is underneath this complex, so tenants don't have to worry about the harsh winters. They also don't need to see the autos coming or going or worry about their children getting hit by a car. You need a key to open the elevator doors, so the children don't find it easy to go to the garage."

"You've thought of everything."

Alicia saw a knowing twinkle in his eyes as he replied. "Not everything, but I'm learning."

"Hey, Jace!" a woman called from one of the balconies. "Grab one of the bags from my locker and take it with you to that communal hall, will you?"

"Sure thing, Martha," he said, turning and reaching for the locker door of #14. Alicia watched and discovered that the lockers were about the size of small bathrooms. This one also held gardening tools and a folding chair; a bike hung from the ceiling. Only one of the doors had a padlock.

Jace followed her gaze. "Everyone has a locker for personal storage. It's down here by the common area."

"Common area?"

Jace nodded. "That's what this area is called. Every apartment has its own area down here where they can garden or sit and watch the grass grow. And it's easy to access because of the communal area." He nodded toward large double doors at the other end of the courtyard.

Jace grinned with pride. This was his pet project. "Come on," he said. "I'll show you."

They followed the path that wound across the courtyard to the doors. Stepping inside, Alicia saw that the room was huge. A stuccoed cathedral ceiling and tall, Palladian windows created a light and airy atmosphere. Lush ivy plants hung from thick, natural beam rafters, along with bags of potatoes and onions and garlands of garlic and peppers. The room smelled of fresh vegetables, damp earth and savory herbs. Alicia felt as if she were a hundred miles away from the city.

Jace disappeared behind a stuccoed wall. She followed him into a large kitchen. Brass pots and pans hung from large hooks attached to the lower ceiling. The commercial stove held eight burners and a large grill as well as a spit.

"Looks big enough to roast a pig." Alicia was awed.

"There are thirty-six apartments. Three times a week assigned apartments cook dinner for everyone. The cost of the food is charged, then divided by however many eat. The meals are eaten here and a social hour of games, TV, sewing and small talk usually goes on afterward."

Alicia was amazed. She'd never heard of such a thing, yet part of her yearned for this expanded family concept that Jace had created. If it worked... "And does everyone participate?"

"Everyone except Bennie Smeck." Jace began emptying the bag he'd picked up and putting away the boxed food. "He eats alone and doesn't trust anyone or anything."

She nodded. "And he keeps his locker padlocked," she guessed.

It was Jace's turn to be surprised. "Right. But he's slowly coming around."

She pulled herself up and seated herself on the counter. "Is he an experiment, too?"

Jace's grin grew slightly sheepish. "In a sense."

"How?"

Jace put his hands into his pockets. "Every prospective occupant must be okayed by a committee of renters. When Bennie came to the complex, he was passed as being fine for the group to interact with. It wasn't until later that we realized he had a few problems that were far deeper than we had originally thought."

"And what happened?"

"Well, now that we have him in our midst, we're trying to include him. He's been here three months and began using his garden space this past week."

"How?"

"He planted carrots. He said that way he couldn't see them grow, but at least there would be a product at the end of the season."

"A hermit?"

"A widower," Jace corrected, "who is afraid of having a cat, dog, goldfish, friend or another wife for fear that they'll die before he does."

"How sad," she whispered, barely able to keep the tears from her eyes. "What a lonely life—a dreadful waste of love."

Jace placed the now-empty bag in a holder on the pantry door. Alicia noticed the boxes of empty glass bottles and jars, as well as one or two boxes of crushed plastic containers. "It's not wasted, it's just hidden," he commented.

Alicia couldn't believe her ears. Was this the same man who spoke so bitterly of family and children? "What about your own love? Like Bennie, do you hide it? Are you only willing to grow carrots?"

He stared down at the checkerboard-tiled floor. "I grow everything."

She didn't know what pushed her to continue. She had no hopes of winning. "Really. Don't you hide your love from even your daughter? She doesn't see you anymore, so how can you take care of that little carrot?"

He straightened, his warm, open expression gone, replaced by a frosty look that chilled her.

She leaned forward and reached out her hand. Unable to touch him, she dropped her hand into her lap. "I'm sorry. That wasn't fair." Her gaze clung to him. Alicia wanted to tell him so many things she wished she could put into words. She wished he cared enough to love her as she loved him. She wanted to share that love with him and with their child. But she knew better.

As if in slow motion he walked to her, fitting himself between her legs, curling his arms around her waist and pulling her closer. His look had a strong, vital quality, trespassing on her thoughts and keeping breath from her lungs. His lips brushed hers open. As she leaned toward him for more, he pulled away.

"Are you always going to surprise me, Alicia?" His voice was low.

The question warmed her. *Always*. How she wished he knew the meaning of that word! Unable to voice that thought, for fear of breaking the tenuous connection between them, she said softly, "Surprise is my middle name. What did I do this time?"

"As if you didn't know."

"What?"

His lips brushed hers again. And again. She leaned into him, loving the feel of his mouth and wanting more. Much more. But he was plainly in a teasing mood. As she came forward, he retreated.

Alicia leaned back, took a deep breath and looked him in the eye. "One of the nice things about being older is that you can say what you want. So I'm going to." She saw bemusement in his eyes. "I want you to kiss me."

Surprise replaced bemusement, then his cheeks dimpled into a grin. "Yes, ma'am."

As his lips covered hers, she knew it was going to be the kiss of a lifetime. The kitchen's scent of vanilla mingled with his after-shave. Beneath her hands his hair teased her palms. The heat and firmness of his body against her own made her breasts ache with a need as deep and primitive as the heavy beat of her heart. Her senses were only aware of him.

A slight pressure of his hands against the small of her back made her willingly arch to him. She wanted him. Here. Now. She needed him....

"Hi! Anybody here?" a female voice called.

Jace's low moan of frustration echoed in her mouth just before he tore himself away and ran a shaky hand through his hair.

Alicia blinked several times, trying to regain control. She recognized the voice as that of the older woman who had called to Jace earlier.

"In the kitchen, Martha!" Jace replied, taking another step away from Alicia. His gaze was rueful, she noted. With deft fingers he tenderly readjusted her collar, then turned toward the sound of footsteps.

He looked to Alicia like the epitome of casual unconcern, which was exactly the opposite of how she felt. For her, the world had both begun and ended with that kiss. It was one more stirring memory to add to her collection. It would warm her on cold nights when she was alone.

Before she could hide the tears that had sprung into her eyes, Martha came around the corner, halting at the doorway. She was clearly as surprised to see Alicia as was Alicia to meet her. Martha looked younger than Alicia had originally thought, her dark hair clearly prematurely gray and pulled back in a lush, thick braid that hung down her back.

Her eyes darted between Jace and Alicia, then back to Jace. The brightness of her smile was definitely reserved for him. "Thanks for grabbing the groceries. I haven't had time to get down here and do anything about it."

Jace's smile was one of tender indulgence, Alicia noted. "Still running in ten different directions?"

Martha bobbed her head as she walked closer. From a distance she'd also looked bigger than she really was. As she reached Jace's side, however, Alicia saw how small she was next to him. She might be large-boned, but there wasn't an ounce of fat on her. "I have a slave driver for a boss."

Jace chuckled. "He's got to be a brute of a man."

Martha grinned and her face was beautiful. "He is, but we tolerate him anyway. After all, he tries not to be such an ogre. It's not all his fault that he doesn't succeed."

Alicia listened to the banter between the man she loved and the woman who obviously felt the same way toward Jace. Her heart hurt with the knowledge. This relationship had begun before she'd entered Jace's life. And it would continue after she was gone. Her presence wouldn't have had the profound effect on him that his had had on her.

She covered her stomach protectively with one hand. Everything in her told her to run away and hide. She didn't think she could take much more of listening to their banter. Surely her departure wouldn't make any difference—to either of them?

Her mind made up, she slipped from the countertop and stood on the tiled floor. As she thought, she was a full head taller than the petite Martha.

At least her movement had caught Jace's attention. He turned, then made belated introductions. Alicia was sure he was watching her carefully for a reaction, and was just as sure she wasn't going to give it to him—whatever it was.

She smiled, holding out her hand to the young woman. "Good to meet you. You've certainly chosen a lovely place to live."

"And work," Jace interjected. "Martha is the manager of the complex."

"And I love working and living here. Jace has done a great job in developing a life-style for those of us who have no family close by but crave that atmosphere."

"Is that the purpose?" Alicia pressed softly.

She was rewarded by a gentle glow on Jace's face. Martha nodded her head emphatically. "Jace knew that there were lots of people out there who wanted the feeling of family and still wanted their own space. This complex made that possible."

Alicia turned to Jace, her thoughts churning. If he felt that way, why didn't he live here, too? Why was he so prickly about family and being with someone? Caring for someone? Why was he so quick to deny any connection?

Jace apparently read her thoughts. "I have an apartment here, but it's too far away to commute on a daily basis." His tone was firm, as if he were arguing with someone at the other end of a phone line. "Besides, I already have a family. And Cam is waiting for me now."

Alicia felt as if she'd been slapped in the face. He seemed to be warning her that Cam was the only family he wanted. Like nothing else had, it brought home the fact that she was alone in her pregnancy. Jace hadn't changed his mind about their relationship just because she'd fallen in love with him and gotten pregnant.

Jace placed a light kiss on Martha's cheek. Then, as if expecting resistance, and willing to overcome it with strength, he took Alicia by the arm and steered her out of the kitchen and across the common room. "I'll drop by this weekend, Martha," he promised the clearly-crestfallen young woman, continuing to march Alicia to the car.

She promised herself she'd remain calm and wouldn't make a scene, but only with the tightest of control was she able to keep that promise. By the time Jace had seated her and gone around to slip into the other side, Alicia felt as if steam were coming from her eyes and ears.

She refrained from speaking until the limo had pulled away from the curb and was headed toward the freeway. "Don't ever push me around like that again. Ever."

"I didn't push you around. I led you to the car."

"You pushed me around, first mentally, then physically," she retorted. "I've been walking since I was a year old. I certainly don't need you to show me how to do it. Especially since I taught little ones your age when I was earning money babysitting!"

"Throwing up your age again? Well, that won't deflect my anger from what you were trying to do."

"What *I* was trying to do?" Alicia heard her voice rise. "I think you're crazy! I wasn't trying to do anything!"

"You were asking questions that had to do with my personal life and a young, innocent girl who knows nothing about me or my family. I saw no reason for you to continue."

Her mouth dropped open. Was he crazy or was she? "I didn't ask any questions. You just read my mind."

"You did, too." He sounded as obstinate as she felt. At least she wasn't the only one being childish.

"I did not! You *assumed* I asked, but I didn't. I never said a word!"

His expression was mutinous, his lips a thin line. Taut silence filled the car's interior.

Alicia folded her arms across her chest and stared out the side window. It was all she could do not to scream at the top of her lungs. But there was so much to scream at that she didn't know where to start.

Jace was first to break the silence. "Even if you didn't say anything, you were getting ready to, and you know it."

Alicia knew her smirk was almost tangible. "Now you're a three-year-old psychic? You act like a child and can still read my mind?"

"Don't talk down to me," he growled in equal frustration. Good. She certainly didn't want to be alone in feeling that emotion.

"When you behave this childishly, I don't know how else to act," she snapped. "Thank goodness, I'll be leaving here in a week. I don't think I could take your hot-and-cold attitude much longer."

"You don't know what you're talking about," he stated coldly. "I'm one of the most levelheaded people I know. It's what makes me a success in business."

It was time to take off the gloves. "I wasn't talking about business. It's your personal life that has the problems, Jace. You'll do anything to keep from making a commitment. You're great at pretending you're not involved."

"I'm involved with you, aren't I?"

"No," she declared, tiring of the fight and realizing that no matter what she said, she wasn't going to win. It was too late. Hope prodded her into one last try. "You make love with me, eat with me, sleep with me and talk with me. But we never say anything personal. Emotions aren't allowed to be discussed. The only feelings, opinions and thoughts exchanged in this relationship could be printed in the *Sunday News* under Letters to the Editor."

"Dammit, Alicia! That's not true."

She ignored his denial. "And I need more than that from you—or any other man in my life. In all likelihood I need the very same things your daughter does."

"You don't know what the hell you're talking about!"

"Yes, I do," she said wearily. "And I have just about as much chance of getting it as your daughter does. But I can walk away. She can't. I'm far luckier than most of the women you deal with. They might really care for you, and that caring could tear them in two."

Alicia heard his intake of breath and saw stormy anger in his eyes, but didn't care. She wasn't fighting—she was pleading her case in the hope that when she was gone, he'd remember what she had said and understand why they should never see each other again. She didn't really expect him to follow her.

Tears blurred her eyes. This might well be her last chance to say what was preying on her mind. And she would. She'd say everything—except for the three words she most wanted to utter. Those she would hold in until they multiplied a thousandfold and she could repeat them to their child as often as she could form words.

"My daughter is none of your business."

"I know," she said softly. "Because of the relationship you set up with me, your relationship with your daughter is none of my business. But I do know how a child feels when she's excluded. It's a hurt no one should have to endure. I'm surprised you can't remember it."

"You don't know what you're talking about." His tone was rough, his voice distant.

"Yes, I do," she persisted. "And I also blame you for the problems with Meagan. You're the adult. If you can't get along with her mother, then you haven't tried. And if you can't get along with your daughter, you don't care."

"It's not that simple."

Alicia realized she was defeated and wanted to cry at the futility of everything: her love for this man, the hurt he'd suffered in his marriage and in his relationship with his daughter. "Nothing ever is."

"Listen to you!" Jace taunted her. "Everything's black-and-white. It must be nice to view the world from your lofty seat. You've never been married, but you know all about my shortcomings in that area. You've never had a child, but that doesn't stop you from telling me how to cement my relationship with Meagan. You're the perfect example of a righteous bitch, Alicia. You know it all—secondhand."

Two months ago that would have hurt. But not now. Soon she would find her own answers in her relationship with her child. "At least I don't blame the rest of the world instead of myself, Jace." She didn't speak again.

Alicia spent the late evening hours alone. Jace didn't come upstairs to the penthouse suite. He didn't call.

Alicia regretted having spoken so harshly, but it was too late. He'd never forgive her for what she'd said. And she'd remained silent about what she felt for him.

She was just as guilty as he.

Who was she to complain? He'd given her just what she had given him—no more—no less.

11

TO ALL INTENTS and purposes, the Chicago Bartholomew Building was complete. Alicia had already stuffed her work notes into Kendall's file. Her new assistant also had Alicia's private telephone number in case she ran into any problems with the furnishings or the few goods that hadn't yet been delivered. Or if Kendall needed a good long midnight talk.

She and Kendall had had lots of conversations over the past few days—talks in which Cam played a key part. Apparently both Kendall and herself were pretending that the men could return their love. Fools!

Giving herself a mental shake, Alicia sat on the edge of the bed. She didn't know what would happen to Kendall and Cam. She did know, however, that Kendall was one of the best assistants she'd ever had and had asked if she might be interested in becoming Alicia's permanent assistant. Kendall had jumped at the chance. They'd agreed to hold off on a final decision for three or four months. Alicia had a lot of arrangements to make before she could consider hiring another worker. Kendall needed time, too, to plan her move to San Francisco. The first priority was finishing the Bartholomew project.

The lobby renovations were just about finished and Kendall was more than familiar with the remaining details. Jace had approved the plans yesterday. Everything was under control.

It was time to leave.

Nibbling on a cracker, she waited for the usual early-morning nausea to subside. When her tummy felt okay, she walked cautiously to the bathroom and began her usual ritual.

It had been four days since the fight with Jace, four of the longest and loneliest days she'd ever spent. Other than meeting with both him and the architects for approval to order the rest of the lobby furnishings, she hadn't spoken to him. Jace had stared blankly out the window or over her shoulder instead of looking at her, which had told her their affair was no more than a bad memory to him. It was the most painful hurt she'd ever felt. The worst part was that there didn't seem to be any end to the aching. The terrible depressed feeling was waiting for her when she woke up and it went to bed with her at night.

Fifteen times a day she jumped up to run and yell at him. Twenty times a day she came up with another way to announce the miracle they had created together. She planned cute and sassy methods of saying "I love you." She even contemplated luring him up to her bed for one more tender and memorable night of bliss.

She *thought* of it all. She *did* nothing.

Now that it was the day of her departure, she was filled with regret. She hadn't even told him she was leaving.

Deep down, Alicia knew she was right. It was best to do nothing. After all, if Jace had been interested in her comings and goings, he would have asked.

But that didn't keep her from hoping that Jace would walk into her office, sweep her into his arms, tell her that he loved her and that he didn't want her to leave. Then she would smile at his suffering, remember her

own hurts and tell him where he could spend the rest of
his life . . .

So much for vengeful daydreams.

Alicia packed her bag with dogged determination.
Forcing herself to think about nothing but the business
at hand, she separated the samples Kendall needed to
mail to her San Francisco office from the ones her assistant needed to complete the project. Alicia felt lucky
to have her overseeing everything; otherwise she might
have had to stay until everything was finished.

Judging by the many conversations she'd had with
Kendall, however, the young woman had been unlucky in meeting Cam. The youngest of the Bartholomew brothers was no worse than any of the others—
he was simply courting Kendall at breakneck speed.
And Kendall was head over heels in love with him,
willing to chance getting hurt for a promise of happiness.

Alicia frowned at the gray, overcast sky. The penthouse had been home for the past six weeks and she
knew she'd miss it. Especially since the warm decor
she'd created was almost finished. Now she'd never see
it in its entirety. Giving the suite a final look, Alicia
turned out the lights and closed the door behind her. It
was time to leave, before she broke down and bawled.

She had the rest of her life for regrets. . . .

JACE LEANED BACK in his leather chair and stared out
through the rain at the Chicago skyline. He rolled a
yellow #2 pencil between his fingers. It was an old
habit, one he always resorted to when in deep thought.

It had been four days since he'd talked to or seen Alicia. Four days of misery for him, when he was the one
trying to teach her a lesson. She would never question

his relationships again. Yet he wasn't sure who had learned what. It had taken that long for his anger to burn down so he could realize she'd been right all along. The questions he'd read in her eyes and seen in her body language had never been asked aloud. That scared the hell out of him.

How could he be so attuned to another person that he knew what she was thinking when she hadn't even said a word? Determined to face the truth, Jace took a good hard long look at himself. It wasn't a nice picture and he wasn't happy, but at least it was honest—something he hadn't been with himself lately.

He'd told Alicia this was a short fling they should both enjoy, and when it was over they would go their separate ways. But all along he'd known his emotions were tangled up with her far beyond the fling stage. And that was true for both of them. He'd even been able to see Alicia's feeling, in the depth of her gaze.

She'd been right when she told him he refused to commit himself. He had. Business was enough of a challenge, without worrying about tension in his personal life. Until now he'd had no choice about loving someone—he just never had. Not anymore. He loved Alicia with all his heart and soul. She had brought his love out from the shade, allowed it to grow in the sunshine and now he was addicted to the light. Now he was faced with something that frightened him even more than commitment—he had to tell Alicia that he loved her.

She'd been wrong when she told him that he didn't care about his daughter. He loved her, too. And he was just as afraid of being rejected by Meagan. *That* was what kept him from speaking out to either of them. If they said no to his love, what would happen? He'd have nothing.

He had nothing now! The thought stunned him. Then he grew calmer, ready to fight. If he had nothing to lose, why had he already declared himself a loser?

Meagan deserved a chance to know her father. She deserved to stomp on his ego to avenge his absence in her life. And she was going to get a chance to do it.

Alicia had so much compassion and love to give a man, and it showed in a thousand different ways. She deserved more than him and his hang-ups. She deserved the family she wanted, the love of a husband, the adoration of children, a successful career.

He gnashed his teeth. She *deserved* all those things— but she was *getting* him. No one else. Just Jace Bartholomew.

He snapped the pencil in half.

He'd tell her so now. Afterward he'd hold her long into the night. And then he'd come to terms with his personal ghosts.

Jace stood and dropped the pencil into the trash can. It was time to lay the groundwork for the rest of his life.

Half an hour later he learned what real pain was— pain that came from love lost. Love was what flowed through his soul as he sought out Alicia. Pain was the response that blinded him when he realized she'd packed up all her belongings and was gone.

Rage enveloped the hurt, and with one strong arm he overturned the cluttered dining table. Paper fluttered around him like a snowstorm, then settled on the carpeted floor like a blanket. Tears streamed down his face. For the first time in a long time, he'd lost control over his emotions. He gulped for air as his lungs demanded more breath. His heart pounded against the wall of his chest until he thought he would surely die.

When he finally regained some control he saw Cam standing openmouthed in shock. It was too late to matter. Jace recalled that he'd sworn never to allow himself to be vulnerable again. Yet here he was, loving and being torn apart by his emotions.

He was scared to death, and Alicia wasn't there to help keep away that terribly dark, tunneled feeling. He wanted to show his love, but she wasn't there to see it. He wanted to shower her with love and tenderness. She didn't want either.

He needed to scream to the skies until he had her attention. But she wasn't there to hear him.

He might be rich and powerful, but he was all alone. It was too late to tell Alicia the things he'd wanted to. Too late to prove his love. Too late.

It was time to face some fears.

ALICIA WALKED down the stairs of her town home, seated herself on the bottom step and stared at the front door. She'd been home for two weeks and had turned pacing into a fine art. Before dawn was a glimmer in the sun's eye, Alicia was haunting the halls of her Victorian home.

It was the same every evening. By ten at night she'd be exhausted and ready for bed. But when 3:00 a.m. rolled around, she was wide-awake and staring at the ceiling, waiting for . . . something.

During the first few days she had expected Jace to call. Every time the phone rang she leaped for it, alternately praying he would or wouldn't be on the other end of the line.

He'd never called.

Then she'd expected him to show up on her door-step. He would storm the door and tell her what was in his heart. Every time the doorbell rang, she tensed. It had never been Jace.

She'd checked with her doctor the first week home. What she'd known for weeks was confirmed. She was two months pregnant and doing well. Her prescription was vitamins and more rest. Basically she could do what she wanted. The doctor saw no reason for her to worry.

She couldn't tell him she wasn't worried about the baby, but about the baby's father. The fact that he hadn't called or visited was confirmation that he was angry. It was obviously a sin to leave a Bartholomew. She couldn't let him find out that she was pregnant, too.

It wasn't until after she'd prowled the dark house for fourteen mornings that the revelation came to her. Jace wasn't going to call and he wasn't going to come. It wasn't a matter of being angry.

Jace just didn't give a damn.

He'd said from the very beginning that their relationship was a passing fancy. He might even have been looking for a way to end their affair.

Alicia acknowledged that she had endowed him with characteristics that had nothing to do with the real Jace Bartholomew and had gone on to fit everything he said or did into those imaginary parameters. She'd even granted him great emotional wisdom, when Jace had stated all along that he could barely cope with a fleeting relationship.

As dawn filtered through the oval, beveled glass window of the door, she carefully placed her hands over her face.

Overwhelmed by her own home truths, she cried as if her heart were breaking.

It was.

JACE SAT outside the two-storied old-English-styled house for well over fifteen minutes. He needed all his strength to confront his ex-wife and to keep his temper well under control. It wasn't going to be an easy visit. Although they hadn't seen each other in over four years, he'd bet she still knew how to rankle him.

But this was the "somewhere" he had to start in order to put things right again. He had to resolve the past before he could pursue the future.

For the past two weeks he'd walked through each day as if it were someone else's life he was ruining. He'd snapped at business associates, threatened to fire his secretary and had gotten drunk twice. None of that behavior was going to bring back Alicia or change her mind about him. He wasn't sure if his future actions would, either. But fences had to be mended before he could go on. At least he had the sense to recognize it.

Sighing, Jace stepped out of the car and strode up the walk. Sitting still and wondering what the outcome of this visit would be wasn't going to make things any easier.

The front door opened. His ex-wife looked as shocked as he felt. She was even lovelier than when they were married. Her dark hair was shot with streaks of gold and pulled into a youthful ponytail. Her ready smile disappeared as she recognized him.

"Hi, Carol," Jace said softly. Maybe he should have called first. "You look great. Better than great."

Her big brown eyes narrowed to slits. "Thanks. Wish I could say the same for you. You look old." Satisfaction laced her words. She reached for the screen door handle as if he were going to break through. "What do you want?"

"I want to start seeing my daughter again. But I want to do it peacefully. I thought it would be best if you and I talked about it first."

She set her jaw. "Talk to my attorney," she said, moving to shut the door in his face.

He felt his anger want to rise, but held it down. "I will. But meanwhile the courts have already granted me weekends with Meagan. All I want to do is clear it with you first."

She stopped in midaction and stared at him a moment. "Why?" she questioned bluntly. "You're not known for either thoughtfulness or tact."

She wasn't wrong. He'd become hard. At least he'd been that way until Alicia came into his life. She'd softened him, smoothed some of his rough edges. "Because I'm tired of our war. I know we can't be friends, Carol. You have enough reason to hate me. But do we have to be enemies?"

"What are you up to now?" she asked suspiciously. He could tell she was intrigued, but also knew she was as volatile as hell when it came to him.

"Nothing. I'm just tired of fighting, Carol. Honest. I want to see my daughter again, and I want to do it with your help and permission. I think it would be best all around if we could at least tolerate each other. After all, we're going to be parents to our child for the rest of our lives. Who knows? We might even learn to respect each other and our differences of opinion."

"No trick questions?"

"None."

"No custody battles you want to renew?"

"Definitely not. I know Meagan is better off living with you. I just want to be in her life, too." He cleared his throat. "I don't want to lose her, Carol. I want to get to know her again."

Carol crossed her arms. "And when do you want this introduction to begin?"

"Anytime. This weekend? Next weekend? Whenever it's convenient to her schedule."

She put a hand to her head. "Let me think about this."

"Take all the time you need," he said quietly, understanding her confusion. "My office number is still the same." He reached into his wallet and pulled out a card. "Here's my home number, too, in case you need it in the future."

Carol opened the door with extreme cautiousness and allowed him to place the card in her hand.

"Thanks for listening, Carol."

"You're welcome," she said, stepping back into the darkness of the entryway. Her hand returned to the screen, ready to take protective action.

Not knowing what else to say, he turned and began the long walk back to the car.

"Jace?" Carol called.

He turned. "Yes?"

Her voice was still soft, but the message was loud and clear. "Whoever she is, she must be some woman."

He stared at her for a moment. "She is."

"Good luck," Carol said quietly, then firmly closed the door.

He'd need some luck, Jace thought ruefully, stepping into the car. For the first time in two weeks his spirits felt lighter. All the same, considering how far he'd fallen, he still had a hell of a way to climb before he reached firm ground. Well, at least this was a start.

Another month passed before he could finally take Meagan away for the weekend. Now nine years old, she was involved in all kinds of activities, including gymnastics. But she finally had a little free time and Jace spirited her up to his cabin in Canada. He hadn't been there in months. They were going to spend the entire weekend together—whether they wanted to or not.

Surprisingly, Meagan didn't complain when she was told the agenda. She didn't complain when the seaplane dropped them off at the cold, dusty cabin. It took them three hours to clean it up, make the beds and get a fire going in the walk-in stone fireplace. She didn't complain when they ate a meal straight from the cans stored in the cabin. She didn't complain when he won the first game of Scrabble. And when he kissed her and told her it was time for bed, she smiled and went on her way without a word of complaint.

That night Jace dropped off to sleep with a feeling of satisfaction and accomplishment. Despite his lack of knowledge about budding young girls, he could handle this.

The following morning he was sure that elves had stolen his daughter away and left an evil twin in her place.

Her hair had tangles that hurt when he brushed. She didn't like pancakes. She didn't like canned fruit. She didn't want to set the table. She didn't know where anything was. The bathroom was cold. The floor was cold. The cabin was cold. She was cold. The house was dusty and she was allergic to dust. There was no TV. No radio. She hated fishing, wouldn't touch a worm and refused to get into a boat. All this in a whine that grew higher with each word she spoke.

Jace got her message loud and clear: Meagan wanted to go home.

He wasn't sure she'd gotten his message. So Jace stated it loud and clear. She was staying for the whole weekend.

By Saturday afternoon they'd reached a stalemate. Jace had run through all the patience he'd accumulated over the years. He'd also run out of reserves. There was no map, no guideline that told him what to do and how to handle this situation. If she'd been a business problem, he'd have known how and what to negotiate. He'd have been blunt and to the point, explaining as best he could how his decision had come about and why it was the right one.

"Meagan," Jace said slowly, forming his words with care. "Come outside and sit with me."

"Now?" she whined, looking up from a magazine that he knew didn't interest her.

"Yes, now."

Sighing deeply and dragging her hundred-dollar sneakers, she followed him down the porch to the swing. Jace sat down and so did she. They both stared through the pines to the shimmering lake far beyond.

They could have been miles apart instead of inches. He ached to reach out to her and hold her close, cuddling her as he used to when she was little. But first he had some explaining to do.

"I know you probably don't have memories of me, Meagan. But I have memories of you. Lots of them. In fact, I have this idea about a memory bank."

She scuffed her feet and jerked the glider. "What's that?"

"It's like a regular bank, but instead of depositing money, you deposit memories you like or that give you a wonderful, warm feeling. Then when you're low or sad, you go to your memory bank and make a withdrawal by pulling out a few of your favorites."

"Why?"

"To remind yourself that not everything is sad and down. It tells you there will be other good times to add to the bank. And it reminds you how much you love and are loved."

A flash of interest flickered in her eyes as she glanced at him. Then she stared back at the scenery. "Really? Tell me one," she demanded.

Jace watched a bird glide on the current, but his attention was all wrapped up in the little girl next to him. "One memory in my bank is of coming home from work late one night. When I came in the door, I heard you crying. The help was already gone for the night and your mother was sound asleep in bed. You were about two years old at the time. I went up the stairs and paused outside your room. You must have heard me, because suddenly you stopped crying. I opened the door very carefully and peeked in. There you were, sitting in your crib, your legs dangling through the slats. You were wearing pink sleepers and you had your one-eared bunny by your side. And there was the sweetest smile on your face—as if you'd known I was coming to get you. As if it was just a matter of time."

"Think so?"

Jace nodded. "You were so darling. You looked like a piece of pink and white ribbon candy."

He'd earned a smile! A bright light shone in her eyes. "Then what happened?"

"I changed your diaper, then we went downstairs and raided the icebox. You had two bowls of ice cream and I had a leftover drumstick. Then we both dunked Oreo cookies in our milk."

He finally had all her attention. "You still remember what we ate?" she asked incredulously.

Jace widened his eyes. "Of course I do. I even remember what we did next."

"What?"

"After we washed up, we went into the game room and lay down on the couch. Then you fell asleep on my chest."

Her bright eyes twinkled just the way he remembered. "Then what did you do?"

Jace grinned sheepishly. "I fell asleep, too," he admitted and found himself rewarded with a giggle.

"Do you have more memories?"

"Lots. Before your mother and I were divorced, you and I were a team. We went everywhere together. I even took you to the office."

Her smile disappeared and she stared ahead, looking mutinous. "Then you left us and we never saw you again."

So that was it. Jace wondered how much of her reaction was due to brainwashing and how much to a young child's weak memory. "That's not true, honey. I was with you every weekend, taking you home with me and not giving you back to your mother until late Sunday night."

"I don't remember that." Meagan tilted her chin high in the air as if she smelled a lie. Her back was as stiff as her legs and arms.

"Maybe you were too little to remember then. But it did happen. However, you're not too little now to add to our special bank of memories."

Meagan's bottom lip trembled and with a flash of insight, Jace realized that this rebellion against him was her way of both vying for attention and expressing her fear that there would be none forthcoming. Suddenly her past behavior made sense.

Jace deliberately set the glider in motion. Then he reached down and covered both her little hands with his. "I've loved you all your life, little one. I've thought of you at least ten times a day every day you've ever lived. But I was afraid to upset your routine when you were little. Then when your mother and I were fighting so much, I didn't think it was right to bring you into the middle of our problems. And now, when you're finally old enough for us to reestablish our relationship, I feel as if maybe you don't care and don't want to return my love."

He took a deep breath, surprised by the emotions he'd revealed. He'd never put them into words before. It felt damn good. "But I want to fight for your attention until you at least think about me some. I want you to know how much I love you, even if you choose not to love me back. I want you in my life. And this time I'm fighting for that."

Her bottom lip trembled. "I didn't think you loved me anymore."

He hurt for her pain. His own daughter and he didn't realize what damage his absence had caused. He swallowed hard. "I've always loved you, even when you were a five-year-old terror. You're my daughter and nothing you do can alter that. I'll love you when you're old and sitting in this glider, rocking your grandchildren." He gave her hands a squeeze. "That's just the way it is, honey. I couldn't change that fact if I tried."

Two big tears plopped onto their joined hands. A sniff grew into a wail, then Meagan turned and wrapped her small arms around Jace's middle. Enveloped in her father's hug, she clung as if he were a life raft. His heart nearly broke. Her cries in the crisp air echoed his own. Her sobs were his, too. Most of all, her hug was as necessary to him as breathing.

After a while, Jace rested his chin against the top of her head. "Does that mean you believe me when I say I love you?"

She nodded, then sniffed. "I guess so."

"Does that mean that we can start making good memories again?"

She nodded again.

"Good," Jace said. "I want us both to be millionaires."

He heard a watery giggle from somewhere around his chest and hugged even tighter. It was an effort to swallow the lump in his throat. He'd been afraid a young child couldn't cope with the overwhelming feelings he was experiencing now. Apparently he was wrong. "Can we go fishing now?"

She burrowed her face back into his chest and shook her head emphatically. "Just because I've decided to love you again doesn't mean I'm going to catch wiggling, slimy fish with big eyes that look at you as if they know you're gonna eat them. Besides, Mom says you are what you eat, and they eat worms!" Her body shuddered at the thought.

Laughing huskily, Jace conceded that this was not the weekend to fish. Something told him that Meagan had his determination—what others called stubbornness—and that he might as well resign himself to pursuing other activities.

"Scrabble?"

Meagan's head came up. Her eyes were damp but sparkling. There was a smile on her beautiful mouth once more. "You bet, but this time I'll beat you!"

He gave her an extra hug, then stood. "We'll see," he said.

Now if he could only persuade the other woman in his life that he loved her....

12

ALICIA SAT on the tapestried stool in an exclusive boutique in downtown San Francisco and stared at her reflection in the triple mirror. She had come to this store to find a few comfortable outfits that might not look like what they really were: maternity clothes.

Almost four months pregnant, she was tired of wearing garments that popped buttons or cut off her breath. She wanted a slim designer look that felt comfortable and looked terrific. Now she was sitting down because the first impression had been such a shock that her knees threatened to give way. This last outfit had really done her in. The lightweight pants were khaki with a knit tummy sewn into the front. But it was the top that crowned the ensemble. In tan with small brown polka dots, it ballooned over her tummy. Elastic secured the hem.

Alicia stood and stared at herself once more. She'd been right the first time. She looked like an overripe pear. All she needed was a tam on her head and she'd have a stem.

She began chuckling. Her chuckles turned to laughter. Sitting down again on the stool, she covered her face with her hands and tried to fight the hiccups that always accompanied such hilarity.

She wished Jace was here to share the joke. She wished he could be a part of this moment. An overwhelming sense of longing for the comfort of his arms washed over her. Bittersweet memories of their time together assaulted her.

Her laughter turned to tears that streamed down her cheeks and made more polka dots on the tan material.

Alicia had never felt so alone. She'd never felt so lonely.

JACE SIGNED the last of a high stack of letters while Virginia stood over him. Once the last one was finished, he leaned back and rubbed the tight spot between his brows.

"That's it," she said with audible satisfaction. "That should give both of us a few days plus a weekend of peace."

"That's all?"

"How much time do you need to tell a woman you love her?" his secretary retorted.

Jace winced at the direct question and glanced at his calendar. "It's Tuesday. I'll be back on Sunday night."

"Right."

"If an emergency comes up, you can call Brad or Cam. It's about time they got more involved with this area of the corporation."

"Right."

"Is Kendall doing all right?" he asked, realizing that it would probably be Alicia's first question.

Virginia nodded her head. "Kendall has everything under control. In fact, I think she talks to Alicia at least once a day, which is almost as much as she speaks to a certain Bartholomew. With the building completed, she's now taken to the job of office manager like a duck to mothering. I'm proud to say I saw her organizational skills first and knew what to do with them for the good of the company."

"You've got a right to feel smug."

"I didn't say smug, Mr. Bartholomew. I said proud. There's a difference." Virginia was visibly bristling.

Jace raised his brows. "Sorry, Virginia. I didn't mean to imply otherwise."

He saw her relax and Jace grinned. "So Kendall receives a lot of phone calls from my brother?"

"You'd have to ask Cam that question," Virginia suggested, slipping the letters onto her clipboard.

That meant that Cam was serious. Otherwise he'd be talking about this young lady, which he was not. Jace was willing to bet his bottom dollar that Cam would soon have Kendall involved in a different kind of contract—one a little more binding than the employment arrangement she had now.

Jace glanced up at his frowning secretary. "Smile, Virginia," he teased. "I'll be out of your hair and you can run the company any way you want to while I'm gone."

"Just be good to Alicia," she said, staring hard at him over the rim of her bifocals.

"If she'll let me," he said wryly.

"Be honest with her, Jace. She'll take it from there."

"And what if the lady says no?"

"Pretend it's the biggest contract negotiation in your life and start talking. You're a great salesman when you put your mind to it. You can change her mind. I know you can."

Jace stood and reached for his suit coat, which he'd left on the back of a side chair. "Your confidence is gratifying. I hope I live up to it."

"You will." Virginia seemed to have all the faith in the world. Jace wished he had half as much and had a feeling he'd need it all.

IT WAS the biggest binge she'd ever set up. Alicia looked at all the cartons of ice cream and frozen yogurt on the wooden kitchen table, nodding her head as she counted them. Eight, nine, ten. Sliced bananas, a jar of cherries, hot fudge syrup, pineapple topping, nuts and a can of whipped cream stood at the ready. All by itself lay one crushed Butterfinger, ready to be sprinkled onto the concoction she would create.

In front of her was an oval glass bowl, perfect for a banana split or anything else of enormous proportions.

Moving swiftly, she reached inside the refrigerator and grabbed the maraschino cherries. She'd been on the phone with Kendall a half hour ago, and her assistant was on top of the world. Cam had flown into Chicago and proposed. Kendall had said no, but knew that sooner or later she'd say yes. She just wanted to make certain that what he felt for her was genuine.

"Are you sure about this, Kendall?" Alicia had asked. "I'd hate to see you hurt any more than you've already been."

"So would I," Kendall had admitted, her voice growing serious. "One man who fooled around is enough for any woman. That's why I've been in no rush to marry—I was afraid of choosing the same type of man twice."

"And are you sure now?"

"Pretty much so. Cam's even offered to sign a prenuptial agreement that states that if I find him with any other woman, I receive more than half his property."

"That's a pretty serious offer."

"Yes. I'm just going to take my time, though. I don't have to rush into any decision. If he really loves me, he'll love me a year from now, too. If he doesn't, he won't be around. It's really that simple."

Kendall was right, just as Alicia felt she was right about Cam's love. They would marry and live happily ever after. Alicia wished she'd been able to reason out her own feelings half as well. She wished she'd had those clear thoughts just two months ago, before she'd set herself up for this fall.

Determined to leave behind those regrets, she reached for the first carton of ice cream. Before she could scoop it out, the doorbell rang.

"Damn," she muttered; her mouth was watering. With great reluctance she headed down the hall. The image framed in the oval glass of the door stopped her in her tracks. Jace stood there, watching her walk toward him.

After a second's hesitation she continued. Damn him! She hadn't put makeup on today. And the old clothes she was wearing didn't flatter her, either. She silently promised herself that she would not let him know how the sight of him upset her. She would not let him know how much she cared—how much she hurt.

Alicia opened the door. "Hello, Jace. What brings you here?" she asked, hoping she sounded casual and uninterested.

"I'm here to see you."

She raised her brows. "Really? Is something wrong?"

"No. Everything's fine. But I'm sure Kendall tells you all about the Bartholomew Corporation and its ups and downs." Alicia saw Jace glance down the hall, then back at her. "May I come in?"

She didn't know how to say no. In fact she didn't want to. She'd have to send him away soon enough, but right now, her eyes were feasting on the sight of him.

She told herself that seeing him for just a little longer wouldn't hurt. "Come in, by all means."

He stepped inside and looked around the darkened living room, smiling at the airy peach and forest-green furniture against the white of the oak flooring and beamed ceiling and white walls. "It looks like you."

"What do you mean?"

"Oh, fresh and clean. Sunshine bright and yet soothing." His gaze focused again on her.

Assuming a defensive posture, Alicia held the front of her oversize man's shirt away from her stomach. She felt as if she were under a microscope, and the lens was not kind.

Jace was still smiling. "Nothing to say?"

Alicia shrugged, letting her eyes settle anywhere but upon him. "Honesty prevails." A good motto, but she wasn't following it. She took a deep breath and looked Jace squarely in the eye. "Okay, Jace. You've come here for a reason. What is it?"

If he was startled by her directness, he certainly didn't show it. "I want you to marry me."

She felt the blood drain from her face. "What?"

His hands claimed her arms, keeping her from swaying. As he drew her closer, a warm sigh brushed her forehead. She pulled back, forcing some distance between them. Still he held her arms and she reveled in the sensation, even as she resisted. She longed to melt into him and feel his arms around her. But it was impossible. Their child rested just below her heart, and she doubted if he would take kindly to hearing that information. In fact, she didn't want to be anywhere around if or when he ever found out. The thought hardened her resolve.

"Alicia," he began.

She raised one hand in the air as if to stay his words. "Wait a minute, Jace. First you tell me you don't have long relationships with women, then you tell me there is no trust in the world. And now you ask me to marry you. None of this makes sense. Why don't you go back to your ivory tower and leave me alone? This isn't necessary. It isn't even wanted."

"I love you."

She was shaking her head even before he'd finished his sentence. "No, you don't. You might think you do, but you don't. Not really."

"I'm not a child," Jace reminded her softly. "I know what love is and what it isn't. What I feel for you is love, and I know that you love me, too. I want you to admit it."

"You'll wait a long time for that."

It was his turn to shake his head. "No, I can prove it."

"How?"

His gaze locked with hers. "You had me investigated, didn't you?"

Alicia felt her eyes widen. "Yes."

His smile grew smug. "I thought so. Well, I did the same thing. Early on. We both should have known then that we were more involved than we wanted to admit."

"I investigate a lot of people I do business with!" she protested.

"So do I, but that wasn't why I looked into your background. Why won't you admit that you did the same thing for the same reasons? That you were personally interested in me?"

"I don't have to do what you want. I want you to leave. Now. Immediately."

"Why?"

"Because I want to get on with my life," she wailed. She was shaking as the meaning of his words sank in. *He loved her!* But if she told him she was pregnant, he'd hate her. She knew it. And seeing that hate in his eyes would kill her.

"Darling," Jace began again. "You don't understand."

"What?" she retorted aggressively. "That you love me? That you want to marry me?" She snorted and took several steps away from him. "Oh, I understand, all right. I understand perfectly well. The point is that you don't understand. I want you out of here. Now."

Disbelief shone in his eyes for a moment, then anger flared. Suddenly even the anger was gone. "I'll be staying at the Fairmont. I'll be there until Sunday noon. Call me if you change your mind."

Alicia crossed her arms over her chest, her heart hurting so badly she wanted to burst into tears. But she couldn't. Acting mean, tough and uncaring was the only way she could get through this encounter. But the thought of him being in the same city for the next five days was too much. "I won't call. I won't. Please, don't wait for me to do that."

"What difference does it make to you whether I do or I don't?"

She became aware of her slip and answered with a shrug. "No difference. I don't love you," she lied, "but I don't hate you enough to hurt you unnecessarily."

His hands dropped to his sides. "How kind of you."

She raised a shaking hand to her forehead, using every ounce of her control. "Please. Go."

Her words rang in the darkened room as Alicia stared at the floor. Her heart was breaking, but she didn't know what else to do. She had painted herself into this corner and there was no way out.

"Are you sure?"

She couldn't find her voice to answer, so she nodded her head.

Jace took her into his arms, forcing her to look at him. His expression was so sad that it was almost unbearable. "I really love you, Alicia. I don't blame you for not believing me, and I'll take the rest of my life to prove it to you if necessary. I love you." His voice was thick with emotion. His eyes delved into the secret recesses of hers, leaving her both anticipating and fearing his next move.

When his lips touched hers, she melted against him. *This is it!* her heart cried out. This was the last time they would touch. Tears seeped uncontrolled from beneath her lids, she clung to his broad shoulders and kissed him back, silently telling him everything she couldn't say aloud.

When the kiss ended, he wiped away the single tear still clinging to her cheek. "I'm sorry," he whispered rawly. "I'm so sorry. Let's end this pain, darling. Please. Call me."

In answer all she could do was shake her head. Then he was out the door.

It seemed like hours before Alicia moved from that spot to the couch. She curled up in one corner and allowed all the pent-up frustration to flow with her tears.

It was past midnight when she finally walked into the kitchen to turn out the lights. Messy cartons of ice cream were dripping their contents onto the black-and-white-tiled floor below. She'd forgotten all about her craving. Now she hungered for Jace.

Cleaning up the mess like a robot, Alicia flicked off the light and left the room. Her stomach lurched uneasily.

She had a feeling it was going to be a very long night.

JACE KICKED HIMSELF throughout the night for pushing Alicia. Fifteen minutes after leaving her home, he was in his hotel room. He paced the floor for hours. Then he sat and stared at nothing. Now he was drinking a pot of coffee and watching the sunrise light up Alcatraz and the Golden Gate Bridge. Sooner or later he'd sleep. But not just yet. Right now he needed to figure out a way to persuade Alicia that his intentions were honest. She was a very honest person, and needed that quality in her mate. He was it.

Besides, the lady always said no just before she gave in, he told himself. But this time he had a feeling that whatever lay behind the fear in her eyes was enough to keep her from him. If he knew exactly what he was battling, he'd have a better chance of winning. Without that knowledge he just didn't have a clue.

By the time the city had woken up to face the day, Jace was mentally exhausted. From the street far below he could hear horns honking and people yelling. A plane or two circled somewhere overhead in the morning haze.

With those noises came an idea. Anything was worth a try. After all, nothing could be worse than *not* trying to win Alicia. Jace reached for the phone book and started thumbing through the pages.

ALTHOUGH Joy kept the work moving, Alicia didn't want to see it. She didn't want to see anything. Early that morning she'd taken her decaffeinated coffee out to the small back deck and sat and watched dusk turn to dawn.

She was going to have a child. It was something she had craved ever since she knew what the word meant. A child represented home and family and loving. This child's father was handsome, intelligent and had impeccable antecedents. So why wasn't she thrilled to death?

Alicia now believed that ever since she'd met Jace, she'd always known she'd have his child. She just hadn't admitted it to herself—or to Jace. She didn't want to admit that she could be so devious, so in need of a child to love that she would trick a man into getting her pregnant and found it hard to believe herself capable of such deceit.

Now she was caught in her own trap. If she told Jace the truth, he'd hate her forever. He might even try to take her child away.

Explaining what had happened might be the only way out, a small voice suggested. But she knew better. She and Jace had discussed children before. His attitude had always been the same: he didn't want any more.

"Then you won't have any, Jace," she promised, addressing the watery sun above. "We can *both* live in misery, separated by a small, innocent child."

She stared into her coffee cup, unwilling to let any more tears flow over the problem she'd created. The deed was done. Nothing could be changed.

Alicia heard the doorbell ring, but didn't move. Joy could answer it just as easily. A few minutes later, her secretary appeared at the French doors. "Uh, Alicia? There's a mess of flowers here for you."

Glancing up, Alicia smiled. "How much is 'a mess'?" she teased. She doubted the flowers were from Jace. Customers sent them as thank-yous all the time.

Joy's answer came promptly. "Twelve baskets full."

"Twelve?"

Joy nodded, and Alicia saw her confirm the number on the invoice in her hand. "That's right."

When Alicia stuck her head inside, she realized what Joy had meant. Large wicker baskets were everywhere, all of them overflowing with bright yellow and black sunflowers as big as steering wheels.

"Good grief," she muttered, awestruck by the sheer volume. She spotted one plant with a giant plastic upside-down pitchfork holding a card and reached for it. It had to come from Jace, and she was dying to know what he had to say. Sunflowers? He had a zany streak of humor.

When the doorbell rang again, Joy almost ran to answer it, leaving Alicia to stare at the flowers that were spilling everywhere. She lifted the envelope flap and pulled out the card.

You are the sunflower of my life.

When Joy returned to the room, so did another delivery boy, holding several pink- and rose-wrapped boxes of what looked like candy.

"A dozen boxes?" Alicia asked.

Joy shook her head, her grin as big as the morning sun. "Eleven boxes of Ghirardelli chocolate."

"Just what I need." Alicia grinned, too. It might be crazy, but it was also funny. Endearing. Charming. And sweet and silly. She was going to cry. She knew it. It was just a matter of time. But her curiosity was also piqued. Why eleven boxes?

The delivery man set down his armload on the couch and held out a clipboard. Joy signed, while Alicia opened the latest message.

Twelve millionaires at your feet. You deserve every one.

Her chuckle turned to laughter. The twelfth one was obviously Jace himself. What a delightful sense of humor! Most men would have tried to be very sweet or very sentimental. But not Jace. Even his cards wouldn't allow him to beg.

Joy let the delivery man out, handing him a tip as he left. Then she turned, bright-eyed with wonder. "Wow, is somebody sweet on you!"

It was a pun bad enough to earn a smile, but Alicia couldn't find one in herself. "I know," she said, her voice barely above a whisper. This had to stop. She had to end this before Jace found out the truth and his love turned to hate.

Alicia headed toward the phone, only to stop when the doorbell rang again.

Joy shook her head. "Flowers, candy. Now what?"

"Wine?" Alicia suggested.

It certainly was. One full case of a California champagne and two Waterford crystal glasses. She was almost afraid to read this card, but knew she had to.

Dinner is being delivered to your house at 8:00 p.m. tonight. Please share it with me. I love you.

Jace had given her the time and place. All she had to do was not be home and everything would be over.

No, her conscience answered. He'd still love her and be hurt. And when he found out about their child, which he inevitably would, he'd hate her. That emotion would reinforce his hatred of all women—including his own child.

It wasn't right. It certainly wasn't fair. It wasn't even expedient. As long as Jace thought he loved her, he would *not* leave her alone. The moment he realized how she had tricked him, he could get over her.

Tears filled her eyes. *Damn these crazy maternity-type hormones!* she thought in frustration, striving for control. Once Jace was over her, he'd find someone else; someone like Martha at the apartment complex. And they could live happily ever after.

"Joy, can you take care of things for the rest of the day?" Alicia called as she walked up the stairs to her room.

"Sure."

"Good. I'll see you tomorrow."

"Okay. Have a nice evening!" Joy replied just as Alicia closed her bedroom door.

Right now she needed sleep more than anything else. She required sharp wits if she was going to face Jace with the truth tonight....

AT PRECISELY eight-fifteen Alicia reached for the doorknob, knowing Jace stood on the other side. She was wearing one of her loose sundresses and hoped he wouldn't comment on her choice of clothing.

Now that she had finally gotten some sleep and realized the consequences of her actions, she was even more anxious to get this over. If she could have run, she would have. If she could have hidden herself from him, she would have done so. However, she'd finally realized that because of her job and his position in the business world, sooner or later they would run into each other again, and he might even hear rumors about her child. That would be the height of cruelty. It was her job to tell him, not his to accuse.

When the door opened, Alicia felt her breath catch in her throat. Jace was in a blue knit shirt with dark gray slacks. He looked so handsome her heart almost broke. But it was his gaze that really snared her. His deep blue eyes stroked her body from head to foot before returning to speak silently to her heart. He did love her; she could see it in his eyes. It made this meeting even harder to bear. Perhaps, if she had told him of her pregnancy early on . . .

"You're beautiful, Alicia." His voice flowed like dark whiskey.

"Thank you," she murmured, afraid to say more in case she started crying again. She'd been doing enough of that lately. In fact, it seemed that that was all she *could* do well.

She led him into the dining room where the table was set. Pale peach dishes were surrounded by gleaming silver and crystal. Silver platters and steamy glass covers were scattered over the table surface.

She stood nervously in the entryway, not sure what to do, all her well-laid plans forgotten. This would probably be the last time she saw him. "Would you care for a glass of wine?"

He smiled. "No thanks."

"Anything else?"

"Plenty," he said ruefully. "But I'm not sure you're ready to hear it."

She turned and walked toward the dining-room table. "I'll ignore that."

"Why?" Jace was immediately behind her, she knew; every fibre of her being was attuned to his movements.

"Please," she began. "Let's not confront each other right now."

Jace's hand touched her shoulder and she responded to the light pressure of his hand. "Now, Alicia," he told her softly but firmly. "I've waited all this time for you to tell me what I've done wrong. You walked out on me and our unfinished business when you left Chicago without giving me warning. It wasn't right and it's not fair." His fingertips tenderly stroked her cheek. "What made you run? Was it me? Something else? Someone else?"

There was no time to prepare a lie, no time to prevaricate. But even given time, she doubted she'd think of anything to say.

"Jace," she began again, reaching up to cover the hand on her shoulder. "I want you to understand that when I met you I had no idea we'd become so . . ."

"Close?" Jace asked with a smile.

"Involved," Alicia corrected. "And I never planned this. Never."

"I know that, Alicia. You're too honest and too upfront to try the usual tricks. But I wanted you. You intrigued me beyond anything I'd ever known before. I pursued you, remember?"

"Jace," Alicia said for the second time, her heart dropping to her toes. He was making it impossible for her to get out of this gracefully. He was never going to believe in anyone again, let alone in another woman. "I didn't consciously plan it. Honest. It was an accident, but there's nothing I will do about it now."

Jace's grin widened. "Is this a riddle, darling?"

She took a deep breath and stared up at him, knowing this blow would stun him, would end any kind of an intimate relationship they might ever have had. But she had no choice. "Jace, I'm pregnant."

His eyes went blank. His expression froze. "What?"

"I'm going to have a baby."

"When?" His voice sounded as dead as the hope in her heart that he would understand. She'd known all along. Why was she so surprised at his reaction?

"In five months."

He looked at her closely. "When were you going to tell me? Ever? Never? When you needed money?"

Anger covered her hurt. She had the rest of her life to mourn her loss. "I knew it! I knew you weren't going to understand! That's why I didn't mention it."

Jace's anger was now as palpable as her own. The hand on her shoulder tightened and held her in place—right in front of him, absorbing his anger. "You didn't tell me because you weren't *going* to tell me. Isn't that right?" His grip grew even tighter. "You were going to disappear and not say a word. In fact, if I hadn't insisted on this confrontation, you would have been content never to see me again."

It was a statement she couldn't deny, so instead she silently pleaded with him to understand. His hand loosened its grip, his gaze grew distant. Only now did she realize just how much she had lost. Before she had only dreamed of losing him.

"Congratulations. I'm out of your life." Jace dropped his hand and walked out of the dining room to the front door. "Goodbye, Alicia."

She saw him move away, and with every step he took her pain increased. She deserved this treatment. She knew it. She probably deserved even worse. But God, it hurt!

The front door was opened, then slammed shut. Alicia's knees gave way and she sat down on a dining-room chair.

At least he hadn't asked who the father was. At least he hadn't seen her crumble. At least . . .

Unable to carry her burden of guilt anymore, she washed it away with her sobs.

JACE STOOD at the front door, his hand clenching the knob so hard that he was surprised the metal didn't ooze through his fingers. Damn! She'd betrayed him completely! How could she do that to him? Hadn't he mentioned—more than once—that he didn't want children? Hadn't he suffered enough with one?

But that one is your child with another woman, the familiar small voice said. *This is Alicia's child—the one she always hinted at wanting. The one you ignored her need to bear, so you could have her all to yourself.* The sound of her sobs reached him and wrenched at his heart. He loved her. He loved her so damn much that he still hadn't left her house. He stood there in a dark-ened hallway, mangling a doorknob, instead of hold-ing her in his arms and rejoicing over what their love had created. Hadn't that been his regret with Meagan? She'd been created out of the need to conform to what he'd thought acceptable for an up-and-coming busi-nessman: home, wife and family. Now he had what he'd wanted all along and he was acting like a spoiled child. Alicia deserved better. For the first time in his life he realized he deserved better, too. He deserved the hap-piness he would receive in freely loving his family. He deserved Alicia and their child conceived in love.

ALICIA CRIED until she thought her body would shatter into a million pieces, and still she couldn't stop. Suddenly, warm hands pulled her from the seat and she was enveloped in Jace's arms. Her arms tightened around his neck, her head burrowed into his shoulder and she let her tears pour over his shirt like a waterfall. He tightened his embrace, rocking her back and forth and crooning to her.

"Shh, it's all right. It's all right, darling. Shh," he repeated over and over. One arm held her close while his fingers entwined themselves in her hair, holding her head against his shoulder.

Soon the sobs turned into hiccups; then even those drifted away, leaving nothing but a drained, tired feeling and a runny nose. Alicia was afraid to move, afraid that Jace would leave her again.

She inhaled deeply and filled her nostrils with the familiar scent of him. She craved to smell him every day, longed to feel his arms around her for the rest of her life, but was smart enough to know better.

Refusing to allow herself hope, Alicia stared up at him. "Why did you come back?"

"I never left."

"Why?"

"Because no matter how mad I was, no matter how much I thought you'd tricked me, lied to me, cheated me, I was going to wake up in the morning loving you. Because I knew that you weren't malicious or mean or trying to hurt me. You're just pregnant."

She closed her eyes and let her head fall back onto his shoulder, resting her cheek on the soft fabric of his shirt.

His hand smoothed her hair. "Besides, I believe half of this problem is my fault."

"How come?"

"You're pregnant with *my* child, aren't you?" he asked, a hint of laughter in his voice.

She confirmed it with a nod.

"I believe I was a willing partner in all this."

"But . . ."

"Did you rape me?" he asked. "Hold me at gunpoint until I succumbed to your charms?"

This time she felt the bubble of hope that had been born when his arms encircled her. It seemed to focus on the area around her heart. But she still wasn't sure. She shook her head in answer, still afraid. What if she was wrong? What if he was just concerned and not really forgiving?

Jace's eyes caressed her face. "If not, Alicia, then I must have been willing. And I never checked with you about birth control. I just assumed you'd taken over that duty."

Alicia placed a finger over his full lips to silence him. He kissed the tip of her finger and waited.

She had to ask the questions that gave her answers. Not knowing his motives was worse than knowing she had lost. "This is all wonderful, Jace, and I love hearing you confess that this isn't my fault entirely, although I know better. But why are you telling me this? What do you hope to achieve by confessing your part in our child's life?"

Jace sighed heavily. "Since you left Chicago, I had to take a good long look at myself and the choices I've made in relationships over the years. Then I had to decide if I wanted to continue that way for the rest of my life."

"And what was your decision?"

"That I wanted more from life than I had before. I wanted my daughter back in my life, and I wanted a relationship that made me feel content and happy. In short, I wanted *you*."

Alicia hesitated to allow her happiness free rein yet. "Don't decide hastily, Jace," she warned. "Our relationship won't be all sweetness and roses. We're both too headstrong and opinionated for that. Besides, there's still a million and one problems to work out."

"I know, darling. But for better or worse I want you with me. By my side. I want to be a part of your life if you'll let me."

The bubble around her heart burst and escaped in a smile. She felt light-headed with happiness. "That's what I want, too."

Jace's laughter swirled around her, his arms holding her in a hug that was as warm as it was loving. "Finally. The lady says yes."

He saw dimples appear in her cheeks as she stroked the side of his jaw. "That doesn't mean the lady will always say yes."

"I know that, darling. But you committed yourself to the most important question. We'll take the rest as it comes."

His kiss held the promise of lasting love, of the warmth she had discovered during their short time together. And her touch answered all those small doubts that still had to be worked out, discussed, argued over.

"By the way, darling," Jace said softly, still holding her in his arms. "How soon can you pack up and move to Chicago?"

She felt the beginning of one of those "discussions" coming on, but knew they would hash this one out until they were both comfortable with the answers. This time they would work *together*.

She looked up, opening her eyes wide in question. "Who says *I'm* moving?"

"Is this where the lady says no again?" Jace groaned.

Alicia shook her head. "This is where both the gentleman and the lady learn to compromise, discuss and decide. Together."

"Together," Jace repeated, relaxing once more. "That's a wonderful word."

"Almost as wonderful as forever," Alicia answered before rising on tiptoe to kiss him.

They would hammer out their problems later that evening. But for now she had plans, and in none of those schemes would the lady say no....

THE LADY
AND THE DRAGON

Dragons were the stuff of legends
and Prince Charming only existed
in fairy tales. Despite her romantic
inclinations, Professor Katherine Glenn knew
better than to wish for make-believe. But when she
came to visit her "middle-aged and scholarly"
friend Michael Reese in his Welsh castle, reality
blurred with fantasy. Michael was twenty-eight,
gorgeous and *never* quoted poetry. His lovemaking
thrilled her but she realized they both were hiding
secrets. And somewhere in the castle of Aawn
something lurked . . . breathing fire. . . .

Enter a world of magic and mystery created by
Regan Forest, author of MOONSPELL, in this very
special Editor's Choice selection available in
July 1991 (title #355).

Available wherever Harlequin books are sold.

HARLEQUIN *Temptation*

LADY

Back by Popular Demand

Janet Dailey
Americana

A romantic tour of America through fifty favorite Harlequin Presents, each set in a different state researched by Janet and her husband, Bill. A journey of a lifetime in one cherished collection.

In July, don't miss the exciting states featured in:

Title #11 — HAWAII
Kona Winds

#12 — IDAHO
The Travelling Kind

Available wherever
Harlequin books are sold.

GREAT NEWS...

HARLEQUIN UNVEILS NEW SHIPPING PLANS

For the convenience of customers, Harlequin has announced that Harlequin romances will now be available in stores at these convenient times each month*:

Harlequin Presents, American Romance, Historical, Intrigue:

> May titles: April 10
> June titles: May 8
> July titles: June 5
> August titles: July 10

Harlequin Romance, Superromance, Temptation, Regency Romance:

> May titles: April 24
> June titles: May 22
> July titles: June 19
> August titles: July 24

We hope this new schedule is convenient for you.

With only two trips each month to your local bookseller, you'll never miss any of your favorite authors!

*Please note: There may be slight variations in on-sale dates in your area due to differences in shipping and handling.

*Applicable to U.S. only.

HDATES-RR

THIS JULY, HARLEQUIN OFFERS YOU THE PERFECT SUMMER READ!

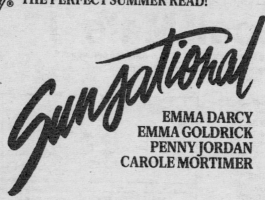

EMMA DARCY
EMMA GOLDRICK
PENNY JORDAN
CAROLE MORTIMER

From top authors of Harlequin Presents comes HARLEQUIN SUNSATIONAL, a four-stories-in-one book with 768 pages of romantic reading.

Written by such prolific Harlequin authors as Emma Darcy, Emma Goldrick, Penny Jordan and Carole Mortimer, HARLEQUIN SUNSATIONAL is the perfect summer companion to take along to the beach, cottage, on your dream destination or just for reading at home in the warm sunshine!

Don't miss this unique reading opportunity.

Available wherever Harlequin books are sold.